ALSO BY MICHAEL NEWTON

Gideon Thorn

Skinwalker

Leviathan Rising

Ghost Town

Mountain Devils

Soul Slayers

Hallowed Ground

Night Flyers

Empty Graves

Rip Tide

WARPATH

WARPATH

A WEIRD WESTERN

GIDEON THORN
BOOK 10

MICHAEL NEWTON

Warpath

Paperback Edition

Dark Wolf Books
An Imprint of Wolfpack Publishing
1707 E. Diana Street
Tampa, FL 33610

www.darkwolfbooks.com

Paperback ISBN 979-8-89567-613-4
Ebook ISBN 979-8-89567-612-7

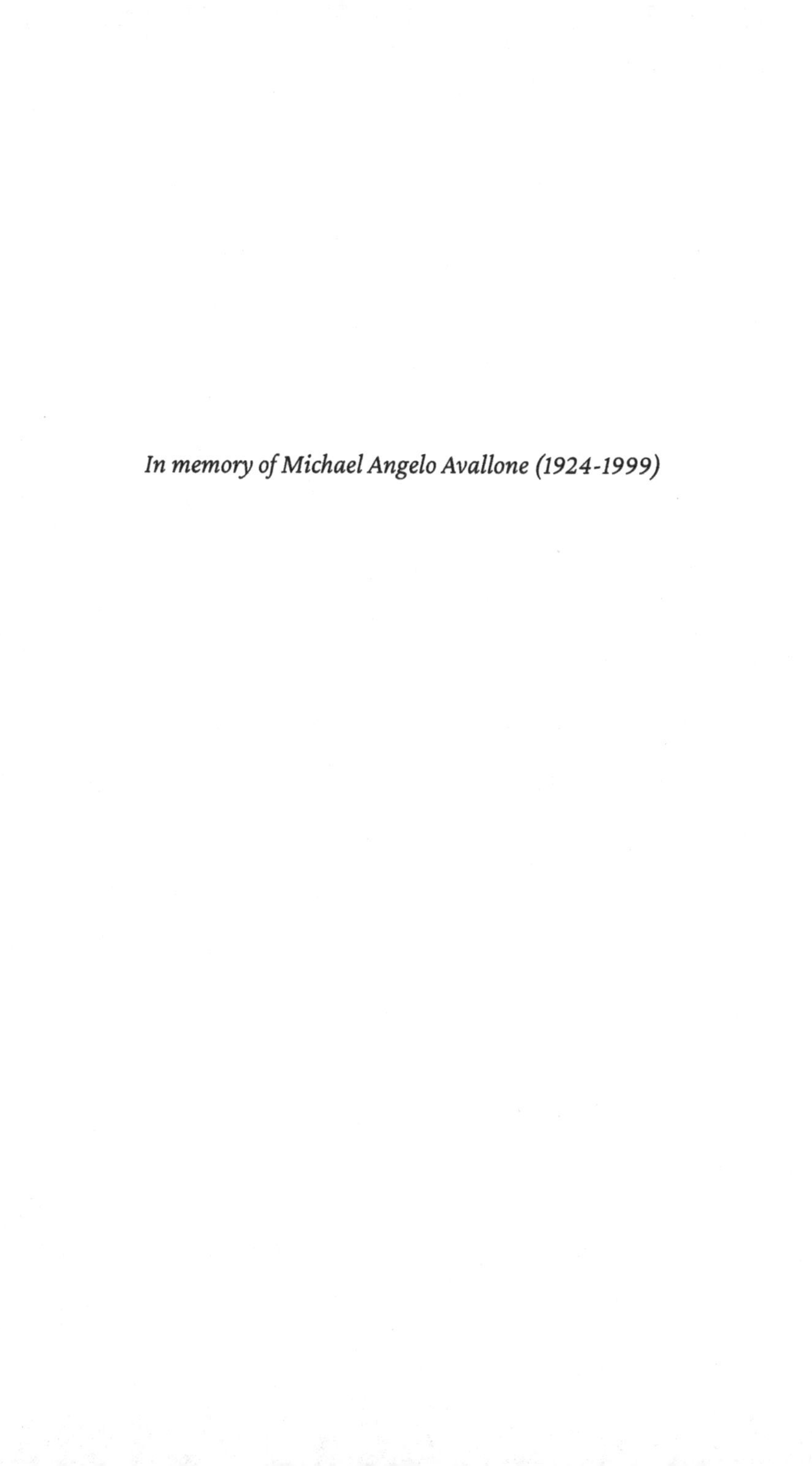

In memory of Michael Angelo Avallone (1924-1999)

WARPATH

PROLOGUE

PIMA COUNTY, ARIZONA TERRITORY: SEPTEMBER 3, 1877

Mauricio Jurado took his double-barreled ten-gauge shotgun with him when he left his five-room farmhouse at the witching hour of midnight. As he closed the door behind him, Alejandra, his *esposa* and the mother of his three young children, called out for him to be careful, but Mauricio did not acknowledge her concern.

His thoughts were focused on the sheep they raised for wool and mutton, animals upon whose health Jurado's livelihood depended in this land that once belonged to his forefathers, lost to the United States in the Treaty of Guadalupe Hidalgo twenty-nine years earlier, when he was still an infant in his mother's arms. Since then, Congress in far-off Washington had formed New Mexico Territory in 1860, then split it three years later with the western half renamed as Arizona Territory.

The territory's name, Jurado understood, was a corruption from his native tongue. Sonora's first inhabitants, before the Spaniards, Mexicans, or Anglos, had been members of the Tohono O'odham nation, translated as "desert people." They had named a region of their territory *alĭ ṣonak*, meaning "small spring," and when European settlers built a mining camp nearby, at Planchas de Plata —"Silver Plates"—the name was twisted by their clumsy tongues until it came out "Arizona."

None of that had any import for Jurado now. He'd built a life and family on desert land where rattlesnakes and Gila monsters ruled before he put down roots, where summer daytime temperatures commonly exceeded 120 degrees Fahrenheit, then plummeted below 50 degrees at night. During the winter months, a high of 65 degrees was common at high noon, dropping below 30 degrees from dusk till dawn.

It was a hard land and a hard life, but Mauricio and Alejandra, with their *niños*, made it work for them against all odds—the climate, rank discrimination by *los blancos*, and occasional outbreaks of mayhem from *los indios*—and made it work for them.

That is, until the past two months.

In late July, a shadow seemed to fall across the land, casting a pall on tillers of the soil, regardless of their race. Livestock had disappeared, believed to be the work of rustlers at first, until the losses switched to mutilated carcasses like nothing any locals had observed before. The slaughter was not traceable to wild dogs, coyotes, or wolves. None would have savaged animals and left them rotting on the ground without devouring their flesh.

And then, last week, the first human had fallen prey to whatever had made itself at home in Pima County. That victim, an Anglo named Luke Dalton, had raised cattle on a spread nine miles from the Jurado property, although Mauricio had never met him. When his corpse was found beside a butchered calf, displaying injuries nearly identical to those inflicted on his stock, concern had turned to panic.

Now, this night, the restless stirring of Jurado's sheep and drawn him from the safety of his humble home—whatever that might be, in fact—to face the wicked man or evil thing that prowled by night.

If Jurado caught a lucky break and killed the thing—or man, whatever it turned out to be—he stood to bank five hundred dollars offered by the Pima County sheriff's office for eliminating it. The payday had begun at two hundred when only livestock were at risk but then the ante was inflated with the death of its first human victim as if lowly ranchers like himself could bear the loss of livestock but the folks in town were somehow more important.

Town.

Jurado almost laughed aloud at that, thinking of Hades—rightly named, in his opinion—ten miles from his little spread and thrice that distance southwest of the county seat at Tucson, but he knew that making any kind of noise while on the hunt was dangerous.

Maybe the bleating from his penned-up flock meant nothing after all, of course. He knew from long experience that sheep were simple-minded creatures, easily dismayed by small sounds in the night or unfamiliar airborne scents but with the *mierda* that had put the county up in arms of late, he wasn't taking any chances.

Not after the sun had disappeared and damned near anything could happen.

First, Mauricio checked the corral. He circled all the way around it, counting woolly heads inside the fence he'd built himself, then double-checking that to guarantee that none were missing, none were down and injured on the ground. When he had finished there, his presence calming them a bit, Jurado was about to tell himself that something ordinary must have spooked them, possibly a sidewinder pursuing rodents, and he ought to get a grip, go back to bed and put a damper on his own imagination.

Then, he heard another sound that didn't fit. Not from the herd secured in the corral but from the barn, some thirty yards away.

"*¿Que demonios?*" he muttered to himself, leaving the pen and moving toward the barn on legs that had a small but vexing tremor to them now. Jurado compensated for it with a tighter grip upon his scattergun, eyes narrowing, although that did nothing to help him see at night, despite the pale light of a half-moon screened by scudding clouds.

Mauricio had built the barn himself, first thing after he'd finished putting up the farmhouse where his wife was waiting for him now, their children hopefully asleep and undisturbed. He'd used scrap lumber and it showed but it was still sturdy enough, its doors secured during the hours of darkness.

And before he reached the barn, Jurado saw that they were still closed now, no indication yet that anyone or any*thing* had crept inside.

Before he could convince himself to let it go, return to his warm bed and Alejandra's open arms, he heard the sound again. Not loud, but still insistent as of some intruder in the barn and trying to get out.

Mauricio decided he could help with that.

Sweating despite the desert's midnight chill, he thumbed the double hammers of his shotgun back, careful to leave his index finger well outside the weapon's trigger guard. His hands were steady now, anger replacing trepidation at the thought of a nocturnal prowler on his property, inviting violence.

Well, in that case, Mauricio decided he—or *it*—could have what it was asking for.

He reached the barn's rough double doors, wishing he'd brought a lamp along with him, but that would only hamper aiming if he had to use the scattergun up close, in an emergency. He kept the gun's right barrel loaded with a birdshot round, for use on desert scavengers and such, but since the trouble had begun, the left chamber contained a shell loaded with buckshot, a dozen triple-ought pellets, each the size of a .36-caliber bullet. No living thing could stand before that blast, much less escape.

Mauricio Jurado hoped that would increase his confidence.

It failed.

Wedging the shotgun's butt into his right armpit, Jurado reached out with his left hand to unlatch the barn doors, drawing one back far enough to let him pass inside. The moonlight had no impact here but he knew where a lamp was hanging, off at arm's length to his left, and found it with no difficulty. Only brooding silence greeted him inside the barn.

This was the tricky part.

Lighting the oil lamp was an operation that required both hands, which meant setting his weapon down, leaning against the nearby wall, and fumbling for a box of matches in the pocket of his faded denim overalls. That made Jurado nervous but, in fact, he got it done without some unknown creature of the night attacking him and took the ten-gauge up again while checking out the barn's interior by lamplight.

Nothing.

How could that be?

Mauricio had not imagined furtive sounds inside the

barn, louder than any rat could make rustling through scattered hay, but nothing in the way of a potential target showed itself. There was no loft inside the barn, no hiding place inside the stalls that held the draft horse used to pull his buckboard and the burro lodged beside it.

Nothing visible, and yet...

The horse and burro both looked nervous, almost wild-eyed in the yellow light his lamp cast over them. They shifted restlessly and maybe *that* was what he'd heard from the outside—but what was agitating them?

No matter how he scanned the barn's four corners, pushing back the shadows, there was nothing to be seen.

Mauricio moved toward the stalls, spoke softly to the nervous animals, trying to calm them down. They watched him, both familiar with his voice and normally responsive to his moods, he could sense that something still unsettled them.

"*¿Qué es eso?*" he asked both of them at once but neither could respond in words, of course. Instead, the horse—a palomino gelding—ducked its head and whickered while the burro simply backed away, retreating to one corner of its stall.

That was the moment when Mauricio Jurado felt, rather than heard, something behind him. He could not have named the feeling if his life depended on it—more a shivering along his spine than anything—and suddenly decided that his life, indeed, might be at stake.

Jurado almost stumbled as he swung around, but caught himself in time, back pressed against the gateway to the horse's stall. He nearly dropped the lamp but saved it at the final second, even as he tried to raise the heavy scattergun one-handed.

There, before him, stood a looming shadow. He could

not describe it otherwise, even if he'd been capable of speech just then. The shape was tall and broad, standing a good two feet above Jurado's five-foot-five, broader across its chest and shoulders. It was man-shaped but of such dimensions that he had to rank it as a giant.

Even by the lamp's light, he could make out nothing of its face, assuming that it had one, and he glimpsed only a bare suggestion of its clothing: bare buckskin, devoid of fringe or beadwork such as sported by *los indios.*

The figure raised its right arm, longer than Mauricio had ever seen on any man before—extended, as he now saw, by a sort of war club clenched within its ham-sized fist.

Jurado squeezed both triggers of his ten-gauge, felt the shotgun kick free of his grasp, and wondered whether he should pitch his lantern at the menacing figure. He might burn down the barn, kill both his horse and burro in the conflagration that resulted, but if that would spare his life, buy time for him to break and run...

Too late.

The shadow-shape before him *shimmered* as his double blast of shot passed through it, harmless, then the weapon in its fist was hurtling toward his face.

Mauricio Jurado had no time to scream.

ONE

TUCSON, ARIZONA TERRITORY: SEPTEMBER 5, 1877

The letter postmarked out of Boston had traveled more than twenty-six hundred miles before connecting with its addressee at the Palace Hotel, on the corner of Broadway and Meyer Street. Surprised when he received it from the hotel's concierge, Gideon Thorn immediately recognized the sender's handwriting and the return address on Beacon Hill.

The epistle read—

Dear Gideon,

I hope this finds you well...or simply finds you, given how you move around. I'm doing well, or so says Doctor Broadmoor. Truth be told, I plan on getting back to work soon on your memoir and am hoping that you might have something new in progress that might serve as a conclusion or an epilogue. If so, well you know where to find me for the next few days, at least. Beyond that, Obi will know where and how to reach me.

Please be safe and get in touch as soon as may be feasible.

Fondest regards,

Dinah

Dinah Pilcher that was, who had nearly lost her life on two of Thorn's adventures and had risked her sanity on top of that. Oppressed by guilt, he had assumed responsibility for her recovery, assisted by the best physicians found in Boston, that city's foremost alienist, referred to in her letter. Only he knew all about the last occurrence that had tested Dinah's mind up to its limits and beyond.

Now she was going back to work—meaning the art of journalism—and was wondering if Thorn had something else on tap to test them both.

That seemed a bad idea to Gideon but who was he to make that choice in her behalf?

Yes, who indeed?

Of course, he felt responsible for all she'd suffered on the two jobs where she had accompanied him into an investigation on the far side of reality as "normal" people understood that term.

Thorn's journey had begun in childhood, when an unknown beast savaged his family, killing his parents and his elder brother. Gideon survived, the only token of that night a long scar on his scalp that left a white streak down the center parting of his jet-black hair. Survival was the key and he owed that, together with his later education, to his aunt, Drusilla Thorn, deceased now, who had put him through the best schools that her father's ever-growing fortune could provide.

Another part of Gideon's survival was the training he'd received in several forms of martial arts from Aunt Drusilla's servant, West African native Obi Magoro, who now oversaw the Thorn family's empire from Boston with assistance from a first-rate firm of lawyers and accountants. In Gideon's absence, Obi had supervised Dinah's recovery, consulting often with her various physicians, trying not to draw them into Thorn's pursuits out west.

When Aunt Drusilla passed, Gideon had been summering in Europe, prior to moving on from Harvard University to its prestigious law school but he'd changed course overnight, deciding that a portion of the wealth that he'd inherited should be invested in pursuing answers to the riddle of his family's annihilation—and whatever other unsolved mysteries he happened to uncover in the process.

It had been a long road, fraught with peril from all sides. Some of the cases Gideon investigated led to "normal" explanations, whether simple hoaxes or bizarre illicit actions on the part of people who had lived among their frontier neighbors without being found out for their ghoulish crimes.

At least, until Thorn came along.

In other cases, like the ones he'd worked with Dinah Pilcher from their meeting to the job that almost cost her life and sanity, there'd been no natural solution that the Wild West's residents would readily accept.

She'd missed his last, most recent case, which forced Thorn into a confrontation with a monster from a bygone age, along the might Mississippi River and compelled him to defeat it with an ex-slave and a submarine that last saw action in the War Between the States. What waited for him next, in Arizona Territory?

Thorn was not prepared to guess until he'd reached a desert town called Hades and reviewed the evidence himself.

As usual, he'd been attracted to the area by clippings

gleaned from newspapers along his route of travel from the town of Natchez, Mississippi, westward. Details had been vague so far, regarding mutilation deaths of livestock which the local ranchers blamed on "something" unexplained, outside the realm of normal predators and scavengers. It seemed worth checking out, at least, and then this morning's issue of the *Tucson Daily Citizen* had noted the first human death since Pima County's rash of livestock deaths and mutilations had begun two months ago.

Gideon folded Sarah's letter back into its envelope and stowed it in a pocket of his black frock coat, matched to his wide-brimmed, low-crowned hat, his vest, and slacks. Even his slim string tie was black. The only deviation in his wardrobe was the white dress shirt worn underneath his coat and vest.

Thorn had been told, on more than one occasion, that his choice of garb evoked the image of an undertaker but he didn't mind. The jobs he undertook, in fact, began and ended with disturbing deaths.

While others, as he'd learned from grim experience, were well-deserved.

Thorn did not view himself as an avenger, certainly no lawman. Truth be told, he often lived and worked at odds with sheriffs, marshals, constables and such—not from disdain for their profession but because the ones who'd heard of him, or who discovered his commitment to investigating unsolved cases on their patch, resented a "civilian" butting in, perhaps embarrassing them if he cut through riddles they had been unable to explain.

Missouri, two years back, had been a case in point. Thorn had arrived to sniff around a series of murders and, in the process, had revealed a family of inbred cannibals who filled their larder with the flesh settlers. In the end, he'd killed a couple of the human beasts himself and seen the last one hanged by order of a local court. His reward for cleaning up that mess, after his testimony was recorded and the last surviving member of the tribe mounted the gallows, was a stern official order to leave town and not come back.

That job had been among Thorn's "normal" ones, meaning that only human beings were involved but others strained the limits of credulity, convincing him that many things about the Planet Earth were still unknown and some of them, perhaps, were better left that way.

Except that, once he'd started on his quest to solve unanswered questions from his past, Thorn couldn't stop.

Last summer, only nine months earlier, he'd tracked and killed the beast that slew his parents and his only sibling—or, at least, he'd put paid to the only member of its species that he'd found so far. Obi Magoro had assisted in that task, one of his few trips west from Boston since he'd taken charge of Gideon's estate, and Dinah Pilcher also played a crucial role in that denouement of that nagging lifelong mystery. She'd done her part in mortal combat and survived, then later parted ways with Thorn and wound up on her own in Arkansas, chasing a lead that almost cost her life and sanity in one fell stroke.

But she was better now, according to their correspondence and the medical reports that Gideon received from Obi on a monthly basis. She was getting back to work—meaning investigative journalism, her first love—and asking whether Gideon had any task on hand that suited her.

Thorn wasn't sure how he should answer that just now and so decided, on the spot, that he would put off his response until he'd reached Hades—that image almost made him smile—and then decide if there was anything in Pima County that might pique her interest, maybe help get Dinah back to work without endangering her life once more.

It might come down to a coin toss, he realized. On one hand, maybe there was nothing to the stories he had read so far beyond a rogue bear or a mountain lion running short of its accustomed prey.

But, on the other hand, if Gideon was pitched into another contest with the supernatural, it might be wise to steer Dinah away from that, even if it meant lying to her about what was going on.

From Latin class at Harvard, Thorn knew that the first usage of "supernatural" had literally meant "above nature"—taken in the days of ancient Rome to mean something divine or heavenly, bestowed upon the Earth by God. These days, as he had learned from Aunt Drusilla's forays into spiritualism, the adjective was more often employed with reference to ghosts and any other entities beyond the ken of 19th-century science.

Thorn had encountered some of those, himself, and had come close to dying in the process more than once. That was a risk he took upon himself but was he ready yet to risk the life or soul of Dinah Pilcher on his own behalf?

Fortunately, Gideon knew no immediate response was necessary. Dinah's letter had been chasing him for weeks across country and, even if he chose to telegraph an answer back to Boston, it could wait a while.

He had no feeling for the Pima County job as yet, beyond a sense that it was time for him to leave Tucson and start the last leg of his journey before losing any further daylight on this Wednesday morning when he still had miles to go.

TWO

LEAVING TUCSON: SEPTEMBER 6, 1877

Thorn tried to travel light while he was on the road, although it never quite worked out that way. After he'd settled up his hotel tab and double-checked his room for anything he might have left behind, he walked three blocks to reach the livery and claim his animals, together with the gear he'd left in storage for an added fee.

At that, he was a walking arsenal since Gideon did not believe in placing any of his weapons far beyond his reach at any given time. He wore twin Colts, the Single Action Army model also known as Peacemakers, and he also had a twelve-inch Bowie knife sheathed on his belt, around in back. The handle of a smaller dagger, double-edged and razor-sharp, protruded from a scabbard tucked inside his right-hand boot, where he could reach it quickly without bending at the waist.

The real surprise, to people passing Thorn along the street, would be his two long guns. His right hand gripped a lever-action Winchester Model 1873, chambered for the same .44-40 rounds that fed his two Colts. Between the three guns, in a pinch, he could fire twenty-two shots without stopping to reload and it had never taken him that many rounds—not yet, at least—to settle any disagreement he encountered on the trail.

Thorn's other rifle was a Sharps Model 1872, chambered in .52-90, a single-shot weapon wrapped in buckskin, concealing its custom-made telescopic sight that measured roughly two-thirds of its barrel's length. Using the scope, Thorn found that he could usually hit a man-sized target at a range of better than one thousand yards.

Most people called the Sharps a buffalo gun but Gideon had never used the piece for hunting game. The root of that decision was a quirk or talent he'd discovered during early childhood, the ability to silently communicate with certain animals—excluding insects and the like—though not in anything resembling spoken words. When he reached out to "touch" a mammal, bird or reptile, if the creature seemed amenable to sharing with him, he received selected images and what he took to be a sampling of the feelings that an animal experienced, including fear and anger, the impulse toward fight or flight.

His Aunt Drusilla had been fascinated by Thorn's talent when he shared it with her, not the least bit skeptical, but rather testing him to see if he could make contact with former living humans on the "Other Side," as she described her concept of an afterlife. That never worked for Gideon and, while he'd sensed Drusilla's disappointment, she had never voiced it openly and sought out instances where he could try to "touch" dogs, cats, pigeons and squirrels in a park, even the rodents lurking in the basement of their manor house on Beacon Hill.

As he approached the livery, Thorn reached out with

his mind to rouse his animals and found them having oats for breakfast, ready to be out and on their way to Hades, facing whoever and whatever might greet them there.

His horse was a gray stallion Gideon called Shadow, strong and spirited. His molly pack mule, Belle by name, had a more sanguine disposition but without the common balkiness displayed by many others of her species. Although equipped with female genitalia, Belle was born sterile like most other mules—offspring of a male donkey and a female horse—thereby eliminating any draw between herself and Shadow at the normal monthly intervals.

The hostler, who had simply introduced himself as Jeremiah at their first meeting, helped Gideon pack up his gear and load it onto Belle, while Thorn himself saw to his stallion's saddling, getting the Winchester, his canteen and saddlebags all squared away. The bill was reasonable and he put a healthy tip on top of it, accepting Jeremiah's thanks with a firm handshake.

If his map was accurate, he should find Hades situated twenty-five miles south-southwest of Tucson. Call it four hours and change if he maintained an easy pace for Belle and Shadow through the morning heat and early afternoon. Basic research had informed him that the town had claimed 417 inhabitants within its posted limits at the last census, conducted seven years ago, although it might have gained or lost some citizens since then. Surrounding farms and ranches weren't included in that headcount but the county had reported 5,716 year-round residents in 1870, expected to roughly triple by the next census, three years hence. That wasn't carved in stone, of course. Thorn was no great statistician but the figures told him Pima County harbored roughly fifty-seven residents for each of its 9,189 square miles.

Naturally, close to half of those resided in Tucson, the county seat, which told him that strange things—the kind that drew Thorn to a given area—were more likely to happen in the county's hinterlands. In Hades, for instance, with its scattered spreads beyond the town's limits.

On such a landscape, Gideon had learned, almost anything could happen.

Even with that in mind, Thorn's outlook was not bleak. Even as a yearling, he had loved America's wild places, from his Rocky Mountain birthplace—part of Kansas Territory then, now Colorado and a full-fledged state since August of last year—across the width and breadth of a dynamic continent that had it all if someone cared to travel far enough and see. The crowded East had shaped Thorn into who he was, firm roots still planted in the heart of Boston's affluence, but he felt more at home on horseback, crossing plains and deserts, fording streams and mighty rivers, seeking mysteries among the West Coast's redwood forests or the Dixie swampland.

Gideon was certain he would never tire of that. And if it killed him in the end, whenever that might be—well, at the very least, no one could say he had not seen it all and done his level best to rid the land of certain predators who had outlived their time.

Engrossed in memories and possibilities, he was surprised to see a weathered sign ahead that cautioned him "HADES, 1 MILE." Thorn had to smile at that, imagining how pilgrims making a religious quest must feel when that announcement slapped them in the face. Upon arrival, he might find the time to ask how founders of the town had picked its name...or maybe inspiration for it would be obvious.

As Hades rose out of the desert, mushroom-like before him, Thorn could see it wasn't quite a one-horse town, but still much smaller than Tucson or the locus of his last adventure—Natchez, Mississippi—where the population must be edging toward ten thousand now.

Minus the ones who'd died horrifically while Thorn was in their midst, of course.

Not all his fault, of course, though Gideon had done his share of bloodletting before he left the Bluff City and headed west.

Hades, he saw when he had closed the distance to a quarter-mile, consisted of two dozen structures, more or less. A church spire was the tallest, one more touch of irony considering the layout's given name. By the time he'd reached the eastern limits of the town or village, pick your label, he could make out signs identifying other buildings that defined the single street bisecting it. Hades had one hotel and two saloons, two restaurants, a livery, a marshal's office, hardware store that also dealt in feed, a barbershop that that offered baths for fifty cents, a newspaper office identified by its sign as *The Hades Flame,* and sundry shops on either side of what a sign identified as Easy Street.

Thorn nearly laughed aloud at that but caught himself as townsfolk on the main drag's wooden sidewalks noticed him, some flicking glances his way before moving on, while others halted in their tracks to study him as if the black-clad stranger were an omen of despair.

Gideon hoped not but the clippings he had studied and digested told him what the residents of Hades had been through since early in July. Outlying farms had borne the brunt of it, no incidents in town so far—or none, at least, that were reported in the press—but every resident of Hades must be burdened with the escalating problems of their neighbors thereabouts.

It had begun with livestock disappearing, naturally blamed on rustlers, likely border trash crossing from Mexico or renegades from the Tohono O'odham Reservation that covered nearly half of Pima County's total area. There had been talk during those early days of sending U.S. cavalry from Camp Huachuca but the soldiers stationed there were mostly occupied with chasing Chiricahua warriors and had little or no time for watching over scattered herds by night.

That first impulse had waned when ranchers started finding sheep and cattle mutilated, left to rot with no sign that the killers slaughtered them for meat, their violated bodies shunned by normal desert scavengers. More recently, a shepherd living north of town had fallen prey to someone or something, found in his own barn with a crushed skull and what the *Tucson Daily Citizen* had delicately termed "extensive other injuries."

That victim, one Mauricio Jurado—dubbed "a Mexican" in print—had left a widow and three children. The *Daily Citizen*'s anonymous reporter speculated that they'd have to sell their spread and pull up stakes.

Thorn hoped he'd have a chance to meet them first, acquire more information, but before he rolled those dice he had a list of other things to do.

First, lodgings. On that score, his only option was the Hotel Continental, midway down the length of Easy Street and to his left. He saw nothing about the place to justify its name but had to try it first in preference to camping on the desert flats outside of town.

He hitched Shadow and Belle outside the Continental,

frowning at a small WHITE LODGERS ONLY sign the management had posted in a window corner, stepped inside its lobby, and was greeted by a desk clerk with a mop of ginger-colored hair, a sparse mustache to match, and freckled cheeks. After a startled blink, as if he had not been expecting customers, the redhead greeted Thorn effusively, smiling to beat the band. The name tag on his vest read "Floyd."

Rooms rented for a dollar nightly and the Continental had eight vacancies among its fourteen rooms. Thorn took one on the second floor, its window overlooking Easy Street, and paid for three nights in advance, the clerk assuring him that an extension of his stay was welcomed by The Management, whoever that might be.

Thorn signed the register and took his key, went out to fetch his saddlebags and rifles in, Floyd watching him approach the stairs while trying not to make it obvious. His room was small but clean, with all the basics and a view across the street of a saloon labeled The Prairie Dog. When he had stowed his long guns in the chifforobe, Gideon doubled back downstairs and led his stallion toward the livery, Belle trailing resolutely in their wake.

The stable ranked among the town's more spacious structures, painted bright red at one time but faded to a soft pink now. Inside, Gideon found the hostler sweeping up with a push-broom and humming to himself, a tune Thorn didn't recognize. At sight of Gideon, he stopped and introduced himself as Monte Rifkin, complimenting Thorn on his fine-looking animals.

Rifkin beat the Continental's going rate by fifty cents a night, per head, and threw in storage of whatever gear Thorn chose to leave with him, no extra charge. "I live out back," he said, "and got a boy looks after things if I get called away. There'll be no messin' with your stuff under my roof and you can take that to the bank."

"You have a bank in town?" Gideon asked. He hadn't seen one, riding in.

"Well, no. Figger of speech."

Thorn helped unsaddle Shadow and remove Belle's packs, taking the opportunity to silently commune with them, explaining that the livery would house them for the next few days and he'd be checking on them frequently. Shadow seemed pleased to have some time off from the open desert. Belle, as usual, kept any feelings to herself but wondered when they might be fed.

Leaving the livery, with three days paid up in advance, Gideon wondered where he should stop next. He didn't need a haircut but a bath would still be welcome after traveling for hours through the Arizona heat. He put that off for later when his stomach rumbled to remind him that he'd skipped lunch on the trail. Thorn flipped a mental coin between the town's two restaurants—O'Grady's and Casa del Sol—deciding that he felt like Mexican.

Gideon beat the dinner rush, if such a thing was known in Hades, welcomed by a pretty hostess in an off-the-shoulder peasant blouse and blood-red skirt that reached her ankles. Dark brown eyes gave him a quick appraising look, then widened slightly as Thorn doffed his hat, letting her see the white blaze running from his hairline to his crown.

The waitress kept her smile in place and led him to a window table, eyeballed all the way by half a dozen other diners. Thorn was used to that, between the streak parting his hair on top, his style of dress, the weapons he displayed. Although he could not "read" people as he did animals,

Gideon had no trouble guessing what was on the townsfolks' minds.

Stranger in town and packing iron. Maybe a gambler or a gunfighter. Perhaps an outlaw on the dodge? Or something else?

Considering the trials their community had suffered, he'd expected to confront suspicion as a stranger in Hades. It would not be the first time nor, presumably, the last.

When Thorn ignored them, most turned back to focus on their meals but whispers made their way around the restaurant like fitful desert wind.

The waitress left him with a simple printed menu, then came back with coffee. By that time, Thorn had decided on *carne asada*—flank steak marinated in cilantro, cumin, lime juice, garlic, and a dash of jalapeño—plus an enchilada, rice, and refried beans. His coffee, black and strong, had just a hint of chicory. He savored it and watched foot traffic moving along Easy Street outside until his heaped and steaming plate arrived, together with a bowl of salsa on the side.

While Gideon worked through his meal, finding it all delicious, he considered what his next step ought to be. Traditionally, he sought detailed information on a job he had in mind by tapping the most likely knowledgeable source, the purveyors of local news who stayed in business gleaning inside information on their neighbors and significant events, deciding, once they had it all, which news was fit to print.

That was how he'd first met Dinah Pilcher, on a job in California's San Diego County that had taken them up to the edge of madness and beyond. Somehow, he'd allowed her to see past the psychic armor that he donned each day, as regularly as his undertaker's garb, and they had formed a bond transcending friendship and a shared experience of the unknown.

A bond which, more than once, had put her life and sanity at risk.

Thorn didn't plan on repetition of that grim mistake but he would gladly pick the brains of whoever collected information for the *Hades Flame,* remaining at arm's length if that proved feasible.

As for the local law...well, touching base could wait a while.

The waitress circled back when he was halfway done, asking if he was satisfied. Thorn offered his congratulations to the chef and took a refill on the coffee, certain that when offset by a beer or two that night, it wouldn't spoil his sleep.

As for the settlers on the bleak landscape surrounding Hades, he supposed that most would do their best to stay alert throughout the night, guarding their families and properties.

But against what, or whom?

Recent events—the pointless mutilations and cold-blooded murder—argued against simple rustlers operating in the neighborhood. Beyond that, Gideon was clueless and would remain so until he gained more specific details of the crimes. And prying into that, he knew, would doubtless draw suspicion toward himself.

Thorn cleared his plate and mopped it up with a tortilla, quaffed his second mug of coffee, and departed with a tip he thought should make the waitress smile. He felt the other diners watching as he left and hesitated in the doorway, half-turned toward the room and smiling at them as he donned his hat.

Most of them quickly looked away, except for one old

codger eating on his own, who frowned in seeming curiosity before he turned back to his rice and beans.

The day was cooling down a bit, but only by a few degrees, outside Casa del Sol—"House of the Sun," Thorn translated, and reckoned it was true most days in Hades. From the desert heat alone, he got a fair idea of how the town had earned its name, but there was also something else...an air of brooding apprehension that he'd felt before in other bergs when trouble beyond normal human understanding came to call.

And how well did the man in black, for all of his experience with eerie—even terrifying incidents—grasp how the local townsfolk truly felt just now?

Not very well at all.

An outsider would have to see it through their eyes, knowing their livelihoods and very lives were now at risk from something they had never faced before, which had no common point of reference within their shared experience or even in the pages of their Holy Bibles.

Ranchers on the desert flats outside of town might be the ones at risk right now, but how long would that be the case? Could anyone in the vicinity believe that he or she was actually safe from peril visiting by night? What guarantee of safety was afforded them by bolted doors and shuttered windows?

Maybe none at all.

Could Thorn relieve them of that burden, as he had the residents of other settlements spanning the past four years and change? Or would his search for clarity end here—in Hades, with an added twist of irony?

He had decided one thing as he left the fragrant restaurant. Since Dinah Pilcher's letter had required a period of weeks to reach him, no immediate reply was necessary.

Gideon most certainly would not invite her west, into the shadow of another lethal mystery. Whether he should succeed or fail, a letter back to Boston—even though he missed the sound of Dinah's voice, her face—would have to wait.

As something else was waiting for him, even now, in Pima County's sunbaked wasteland.

Thorne needed more information. And where better to seek that than in the light cast by the *Hades Flame*?

THREE

Thorn had dealt with small-town newspapers and publishers before during his travels and he'd found them as diverse across the continent as anybody might expect. The individuals in charge were steeped in local politics and customs, even superstitions, which permitted them to operate within communities where they survived on advertising fees, catered to certain well-placed individuals with flattery, banking goodwill against the day when they might have to break the news of a scandal that could not be swept under the rug.

With stranger tales, the stories that enticed Gideon Thorn, most editors were reticent to crawl out on a shaky limb. Their hearts and minds were commonly divided between warning a community of danger in its midst versus inciting panic that might do more damage than the lurking threat itself.

Most journalists, in Thorn's experience, were fairly decent people, though he had encountered some who were corrupt and bigoted, together with a few—a tiny handful, thankfully—who verged on being lunatics themselves.

What waited for him now, inside the office of the *Hades Flame*?

A small sign in the front door's window told that the paper's office was OPEN. Entering, he heard a small bell chime, above his head, on impact from the swinging door, and then a man's voice called out from a backroom, "Coming! Just a moment, please!"

The fellow who emerged, at last, was in his early thirties, balding, with a beard to compensate that he kept neatly trimmed. Shorter than Gideon's own six-foot-four, Thorn guessed he would have tipped the scales around 180 pounds. He wore a blue shirt with the sleeves rolled up above his elbows, underneath a plain vest, tucked into a pair of baggy slacks. A pair of wire-rimmed spectacles rode on his beaklike nose and amplified his curious gray eyes.

Those eyes examined Gideon from head to toe in seconds flat, with just a heartbeat's hesitation on his brace of holstered Colts, then came back to his face. The newsman's automatic smile of greeting seemed a trifle hesitant but still remained in place.

"Good afternoon, sir. A newcomer to Hades, eh? I'm Ellis Flynn, proprietor and jack of all trades at the *Flame*."

"Gideon Thorn." He shook Flynn's offered hand across the intervening counter, pleased to find it strong and dry.

"Gideon Thorn," the journalist repeated. "Thorn... Thorn...I should know that name." A moment later, as his fingers snapped, Flynn said, "Of course! I've read about you in dispatches published by my competition, west and east. Just bits and pieces, mind you. Some were quite...*imaginative*, no offense intended."

Adding that last bit as his eyes dipped again toward Gideon's pistols.

"None taken," Thorn replied. "Some of the things I've read, I wouldn't swallow it myself."

"And here you are in Hades," Flynn observed, stating the obvious. "Before your time, at that," he quipped.

Thorn's frown cut off Flynn's laugh. "Sorry again," Flynn said. "A joke some of the locals use on newcomers but wearing thin, I fear."

"A little humor never hurts," Thorn granted, striving for a smile.

"What brings you here, if I may ask?"

"I've read about some troubles in the area, the kinds that puzzle me."

"It's true, then," Flynn replied. "You travel far and wide in search of"—hesitation for another heartbeat there, Flynn winding up with—"mysteries."

In that split second, Gideon had wondered if the last word would be "monsters."

"More or less," he granted.

"And find solutions for them on occasion, I believe some of the stories said?"

"Solutions of a sort."

"And coming here—to speak with me, I mean—you hope to glean...?"

"More detailed information than I picked up from the *Tucson Daily Citizen*," Thorn said.

"Ah, yes. They may speak for the county seat but sometimes they play fast and loose with facts. I've seen their copy on our late unpleasantness. If one of their reporters ever came to Hades, I'd would be surprised. I guarantee none ever spoke with me."

"And that's the kind of local insight that I'm missing," Thorn allowed.

"Well, sir, you've come to the right place. I'll help you if I can and, in return—"

Gideon knew were Flynn was going. Cut him off with, "I'd prefer to skip the interviews, for now, at least until I get a better feel for what's been going on."

"I understand completely, Mr. Thorn. But after your investigation is concluded..."

Gideon was tempted to reply, *Assuming that it ever is. Assuming I'm alive.*

Instead, he answered, "Then we'll talk."

"On record?"

Thorn considered that. Said, "I'll be straight with you but I can't promise that you'll want to print it."

Frowning now, Flynn told him, "Fair enough. Now, as to what you're looking for..."

"Whatever you can tell me, from the first attacks on animals and going on from there."

"Yes, yes." Flynn opened up a small gate in the counter, holding it for Thorn. "If you'll just step into my morgue."

Thorn wasn't sure he liked the sound of that but understood the jargon of Flynn's trade. He cleared the gate and told his host. "Lead on."

Flynn's "morgue" consisted of some shelves along one office wall, the uppers lined with bound and dated volumes of the *Hades Flame* that spanned three years, presumably since Flynn established the newspaper or took charge of it from someone else. The lower shelves were stacked with neatly folded issues of the paper, forming piles of twenty-five to thirty each.

"The *Flame* is a bi-weekly," Flynn explained. "Call it eight issues monthly, more or less."

"And these attacks date back three months, I understand," Floyd said.

"Correct."

The publisher moved to the right-hand shelves, least heavy-laden of the lot, and grabbed a stack of thirty issues, more or less, returning with them to his desk. He set them on a corner of the desktop, cleared off some unfinished sheets of foolscap bearing neat handwriting that Thorn didn't bother reading upside-down.

"June's on the top," Flynn said, "but I can talk you through the sequence of what's happened while you read, if that's all right?"

"Appreciate it," Gideon allowed.

"Go on and take my chair. I need to stretch my legs.

Thorn sat. Flynn moved the first June issue of the *Flame* aside and placed the one beneath it in Thorn's hands.

"The trouble started on June ninth," Flynn said, "but no one recognized it right away. Gabe Whitfield lost two head of cattle on his place northwest of town, just up and gone. No trace of any violence, so rustlers got the blame for that."

"Makes sense," Thorn granted as he scanned the *Flame*'s short page-two article.

"Our marshal poked around but came up empty handed. Figured that whoever took the steers were keeping them at home or had already run them down to Mexico."

"That's not much of a raid," Thorn mused. "Two head."

"I wondered about that," said Flynn, "but if it was a local...well, who knows?"

"Okay."

"Next up, Adolphus Meyer. He got hit for five steers, leaving one behind. His place is five miles south of town, about as far as you can go from Whitfield's and still count as living in the Hades area."

"And closer to the border," Thorn said.

Flynn was nodding. "That was what our marshal

thought, as well. He telegraphed the sheriff, up in Tucson, but they couldn't spare a man."

Thorn skimmed the second article, a longer one, and moved up to page one below the fold. Again, no clues discerned.

"The third time fell on Independence Day," Flynn said. "While folks were setting fireworks off on Easy Street, someone—or something—made a run at Evan Montague's sheep ranch, due east of Hades. No stock disappeared that time but fifteen out of twenty-five he had on hand were torn apart, the pieces scattered far and wide. He found the five survivors in a state of shock. One of them died the next day, like its heart just up and quit."

"That's major escalation," Gideon observed.

"And no one gave a passing thought to rustlers after that raid."

"Did this Montague have enemies?"

"None he'd admit to but the marshal asked around. Got nowhere for his trouble."

Coverage of that strike had made headlines, edging out the fireworks celebration.

"The fourth attack occurred on August ninth," Flynn said. "Griff Stevens is a small-time cattleman, lives nine or ten miles west of town. Whatever hit his place, it butchered his whole herd—that's thirteen head—and left his German shepherd watchdog dying in the barnyard, missing one leg that was nowhere to be found."

"You said 'whatever'," Thorn remarked.

Flynn's nod was grim. "The mutilations this time...well, I guess a giant of a man, or more than one, could be responsible, but there were no marks of a cutting tool on any of the carcasses."

"None of them mauled?" Thorn prodded him.

"Nary a nip, much less a mouthful eaten."

That attack had taken fully half of the front page, beneath a banner headline asking, "WHO OR WHAT IS PROWLING IN THE NIGHT?"

"Excitement heating up," Thorn said.

"As you'd expect, especially with any town this size."

Flynn let him read the article, then said, "The fifth attack came five days later. Felix Sundberg is the nearest neighbor to the first ranch to be hit. He only had four steers but all of them were torn apart. One of their heads was tossed onto his roof."

"He couldn't see who did it?"

"Who or *what*. He told the marshal that he heard his cattle screaming and some kind of growling noise along with that. His wife latched onto him and wouldn't let him go outside."

Thorn skimmed the article and waited for the next attack, the one that had occurred when he was already in Tucson.

"That brings us to poor Mauricio Jurado," Flynn said. "He ran sheep, had thirty head or so. According to his wife, he heard them fussing and went out to check, taking his ten-gauge with him."

"That's a lot of gun," Flynn said.

"And he got off both barrels of it, in his barn. Ripped up one of the walls before his skull was crushed and he was torn apart."

"The sheep?"

"In a corral outside," Flynn said. "Wild-eyed, but not a scratch on any one of them, except where some had run against the fence."

"So, escalation."

"Bloody murder," Flynn corrected him.

"But only if the killer was another human being."

"What else could it be?" the newsman challenged him. "Our marshal says the blow that killed Mauricio came from some heavy object, like a club. A punch or kick couldn't have done it that way, even from a good-sized horse.

Thorn took his time reading the final front-page article before he set that copy of the *Flame* aside.

"It's puzzling," he said, "to say the very least."

"Have you seen anything like this before?"

"No," Gideon replied. "This is a first for me."

"If you don't mind me asking," Flynn pressed on, "how do you go about investigating in your...line of work, I guess you'd say?"

"Just like with anything that comes along," Thorn said. "I take it one step at a time and see what I can learn."

"You want me to, I could provide an introduction to our marshal, Hardy Ruggles."

"That's a trifle premature, I'd say."

"But if you want to pick his brain..."

"I find most lawmen don't appreciate a stranger butting in, a thing like this."

"Oh, right. I hear you. But if I could tag along..."

"I'll need to get my bearings first," Thorn said. "But I'd appreciate directions to some of those farms you talked about."

"Sure thing. I'll get right on that and—"

"Tomorrow's soon enough," Gideon interrupted. "Sometime after breakfast?"

"Absolutely. Anything that I can do to help."

And get yourself another front-page spread, Thorn mused. He would be fortunate if Flynn's excitement to be part of something strange and newsworthy did not derail his own pursuit of answers at its start. And if Flynn got the local law involved...

Gideon shook hands with the publisher before he left the *Flame*'s office and spent a moment on the sidewalk, sharp eyes scanning Easy Street. Considering the look of stores and offices flanking the unpaved thoroughfare, he had to wonder if the street's name—like the town's—had been somebody's notion of a joke. Looking from north to south and back again, while waning afternoon sunlight cast long shadows before it, he saw only six pedestrians, presumably all townspeople, moving along the street. Some of the stores already had CLOSED signs displayed, to keep the strollers moving on their way to somewhere else.

Hades had learned to live with fear, he understood, or was attempting to. There had been no attacks within the town so far but now that human blood had spilled, along with that of animals, all bets were off.

Thorn was not hungry, planned on skipping supper, trying breakfast at O'Grady's bright and early in the morning, but he thought a drink or two would suit him well enough before he turned in at the Continental for—he hoped—a good night's sleep. A silent mental found of "Eenie, Meenie" sent him ambling off toward Diamond Lil's, the closer of the two saloons in town to where he stood and afterward to his hotel.

The place was relatively quiet as he pushed in through the batwing doors and heard them flap behind him. Three drinkers were spaced along the bar, all drinking beer from mugs, one of them chatting with a painted lady who most likely had a crib upstairs. Off to his left, four men were playing cards—it looked like five-card stud—but took a break from betting to eyeball the black-clad stranger in their midst. To Thorn's right, a piano with a fallboard covering its keys stood unattended, sheet music on its rack awaiting someone who could play.

The bartender was husky, sporting muttonchops, and had a marled left eye. Age-wise, he might have been somewhere in his mid-fifties but Gideon knew the desert aged people before their time. One eye scanned Thorn from hat to boots as he approached, then narrow lips said, "Thanks for trying Lil's. What can I get for you?"

"Old Overholt, a double, with a beer back," Gideon replied.

"Coming right up."

The barkeep fixed him up and made Thorn's silver dollar disappear with no attempt at making change. Gideon took his mug and shot glass to a table on the far side of the barroom from the poker players, settled with his back against the wall, and sipped the rye, taking his time to savor it before he chased it with a slug of suds.

He'd finished off the whiskey and was halfway through his beer before a man's long shadow fell across the barroom floor. Thorn flicked a glance toward the street entrance, kept his face expressionless as he noted the weary-looking new arrival's badge. It read TOWN MARSHAL, limiting his jurisdiction to the city's limits if he cared much for the law. In Thorn's varied experience, some did and some did not.

Gideon watched the marshal spot him, sitting on his own, and make a beeline for his table. Standing over him, the lawman measured close to six feet even, weighed about 180 pounds, and kept his right hand resting on the curved butt of his single Colt.

"Gideon Thorn?" he asked.

"The very same."

"Brett Ruggles. I'm the law in Hades."

Gideon resisted all the jokes that came to mind and

nodded toward the empty chair across from him. "Feel free to take a load off."

Ruggles sat. Remarked, "You're new in town."

"That didn't take long," Gideon replied.

The marshal frowned across at him. "How's that?"

"For Ellis Flynn to tip you off."

"Fact is, I haven't seen him for a couple days."

"So, this is a coincidence?"

"I watch for strangers passing through, especially these days. Saw you ride past my office. Checked the Continental first."

The hotel clerk, then. "Marshal," Thorn said, "I can promise you I'm not behind the troubles you've been having."

Ruggles nodded. "I know that. You wrote your own name in the register."

"I make a habit of it."

"And it rang a bell," the marshal said.

Twice in a single hour? Gideon sat quietly and let the lawman say his piece.

"You make the papers now and then."

"Guilty as charged."

"You come from money. Ride around the country, looking into...certain things."

"And this," said Gideon, "is where you tell me that you don't need any help, I should clear out of town and let you do your job, et cetera."

The marshal's smile surprised him. Ruggles answered back, "I hope you're better at investigating than you are at reading minds."

"Well, if this isn't a brush-off..."

"Truth is, Mr. Thorn, I *do* need help. What we've been through the past couple of months is nothing like I've ever seen or heard tell of before. I talked to Charley Shibell—he's the Pima County sheriff, up in Tucson—says his deputies are spread too thin to help us. I suppose that's partly true but I still need someone to help us now that whoever's behind this took the step from killing stock to butchering a man."

"And what if it's not 'who'?" Gideon asked him.

"I like keeping both feet on the ground unless I'm riding horseback," Ruggles said, "but I've run out of easy answers. Hell, I've run clean out of *questions*."

"I can't promise you solutions," Thorn advised. "Sometimes, I crack a thing like this and sometimes it goes up in smoke."

"But you've *seen* things like this?" the marshal prodded him.

"Some worse. Some come to nothing."

"Meaning what?"

"Sometimes it traces back to normal predators or crazy people. Sometimes there's no answer to be found."

"Okay. I'd rather go down swinging than just sitting on my hands."

"I'd need to look around the sites where all this happened, starting with the last one first."

"I'll take you out there in the morning," Ruggles said. "I've got no legal jurisdiction outside city limits but, since no one at the county seat's done anything to help, I'll stretch a point."

Thorn felt himself beginning to relax. He wondered what it might be like, working together with a lawman on the case, instead of butting heads.

"Sounds good to me," Gideon said. "I planned on taking breakfast at O'Grady's in the morning. We can meet and ride out after that."

"They have an early service for the shopkeepers and such," said Ruggles. "Open up at six most days. Would seven-thirty suit you?"

"Fine."

The marshal reached across and offered Thorn his hand. They shook and Gideon said, "Have a drink on me before you go?"

"I'm still on duty," Ruggles told him. "Nightly rounds and all."

"Till seven-thirty, then."

He watched the marshal leave, detouring past the poker players, greeting them, laughing at some remark from one of them before he left. Gideon thought about another drink, then reckoned he should skip it. Thought about a walk down to the barbershop, a bath to help him unwind from the trail, but then dismissed that notion too.

Thorn's bed was calling to him, early in the evening as it was. In the morning, he'd be getting down to business, whatever the job turned out to be. And working with the marshal for a change.

It almost seemed too easy, falling into place like that, but he had read the lawman's keen sense of frustration, understood the weight that rested on his shoulders from responsibility for every life in Hades. Those who lived outside the town, who'd lost their animals—and one who'd lost his life so far—were clearly weighing on him too. Some other marshals might have shrugged that off, much as the county sheriff seemed prepared to do, but Ruggles had been cut from different cloth.

Exiting Diamond Lil's, Gideon hoped that they could work together and resolve the lethal mystery that haunted Hades like a plague but he'd been honest with his warning to the marshal.

With some jobs he undertook, the pieces all fell into place. Sometimes he failed.

And sometime, somewhere down the road, Thorn knew that he might come to grief.

That was the risk he took and willingly accepted every time he mounted Shadow and moved on from one location to another seeking to resolve a mystery that had confounded law enforcement officers and journalists, church ministers and politicians. When he solved a case, sometimes the local citizens were horrified by what behavior was evoked from neighbors in a fit of madness. Other times, they struggled to accept an answer that defied their understanding of the world around them.

And sometimes, in those cases, they tried to place the blame on Gideon.

But they were wrong.

He was a hunter, not the predator who threatened them...unless, of course, the mayhem sprang from twisted human hearts and minds.

To work that out, Thorn had to do the research for himself and he would welcome any help that Marshal Ruggles could provide.

While hoping that collaboration with him did not get the lawman killed.

FOUR

WEST OF HADES: SEPTEMBER 6, 1877

Jack Conyers, if you'd asked him, would have said he was as capable as any of his Pima County neighbors and superior to some at caring for his stock. Before this summer, he'd have likely said he was as brave as any of them, too, but the events that had transpired since June were testing that resolve.

Ranchers in Arizona Territory dealt with livestock losses as a fact of life. Cattle, in Conyers's case, fell prey to mountain lions, wolves, coyote packs, and one or two per year, in normal times, predictably fell prey to rattler bites. Rustlers were always on the prowl, as well.

Since June, though, stockmen tending herds or flocks in Pima County had not lived in anything resembling normal times.

The early disappearances were bad enough, if still explainable in terms that every rancher understood. The later mutilations, without any hint of feeding on the carcasses, were something else entirely. And the recent loss of human life put everyone on edge around the clock.

Conyers had never met victims Luke Dalton or Mauricio Jurado, but had heard about Mauricio in passing, one of Pima County's better sheepmen, even if he was a Mexican. His murder three nights earlier—his *slaughter,* if what Conyers heard about the crime was true—changed everything. No settler living within two-days' ride of Hades left his house without a weapon to defend himself and strangers who came calling ran a risk of being shot on sight.

This Thursday evening, as Conyers went to bed his cattle down, he wore a Smith & Wesson Model 3 Schofield revolver on his hip, the break-top pistol chambered for .44-caliber rounds. In case that big iron wasn't quite enough to drop a nocturnal intruder, Dalton also brought his Winchester Model 1866 rifle—nicknamed the "Yellow Boy" for its gunmetal receiver forged from a brass-and-bronze alloy—that gave him fourteen shots before he had to fall back on the Schofield.

In the house, its front door barred while Jack was out, his wife, Sonya, was armed with a Colt House Revolver, the Cloverleaf model so-called for its four-shot cylinder loaded with .41-caliber rimfire cartridges. Even with nerves on edge, she knew enough to keep from shooting Luke—at least as long as he announced himself loudly, returning from his tour of the spread and knocked right sharply on their door.

If he forgot that simple rule...well, anything that happened next would be his own damned fault.

Conyers disliked the sense of living under siege after sundown but that was nothing new for Pima County residents. At one time or another through the years, white settlers had been faced with raids by the Apache, Navajo,

Kaibab, Paiute, and Yaqui native tribes, along with bandits up from Mexico or on the dodge from posses out of Southern California and New Mexico.

But none of those had spread fear through the district anything like the oppressive dread of who- or whatever had started preying on outlying spreads since June.

This dread was new and all the worse because it was mysterious, without a source that Conyers could identify or fight against.

Jack's thirty head of cattle were corralled but open to attack and, now that full dark had descended on the desert, he was on his way to remedy that lapse by shifting them into his spacious barn. After Luke Dalton's and Mauricio Jurado's deaths, he worried more about his life and Sonya's than their livestock but, at the same time, the cattle were their livelihood. Not much compared to Arizona Territory's larger ranches, granted, but without them, he would have to start from scratch at age forty—that is, if he managed to avoid the district's lurking predator himself.

Conyers loved Sonya beyond measure and the fact that they had never managed to produce a child still grated on him when he thought about it. But these days and nights, he had enough to keep him occupied without the worry that a child might wander off somewhere and not return.

Approaching the corral, Luke counted steers under the half-moon's light and found all of them present, thirty animals accounted for. They seemed a trifle restless but that could mean anything, one of them picking up on Conyers's case of nerves, the others falling into line with his uneasiness. The trick, now, was to move them out in single file and toward the barn.

In safer times, by daylight, Sonya could have helped

him with it. But tonight, he wanted her locked up inside the house, her pistol close at hand.

Before he opened the corral's gate, Conyers detoured to the barn, drew back its double doors, and went inside to light a lamp he kept there, using it to scan the barn's interior. Nothing appeared that struck his mind as sinister or threatening, only a field mouse scurrying for cover from the lamplight.

Clear and good to go.

Conyers drew back the gate to the corral, spoke softly to his herd, and gestured with his free hand toward the barn, holding the Winchester against his leg and pointed toward the ground. The Hereford bull came first, fifteen hundred pounds of muscle leading the parade as usual, the other steers trailing behind him single file. Dalton stood by to make sure none of them decided on a jaunt around the barnyard on their own. When all were safely in the tucked away and munching feed, he doused the lamp and barred the barn's door from the inside, leaving through a smaller exit at the rear.

Another turn around the property and Conyers thought he should be able to turn in.

As to the quality of sleep he'd get tonight...well, that was still in doubt.

Inside the ranch house, Sonya Conyers kept her mind on busywork. She'd cleaned the supper dishes, pots, and pans before she started dusting furniture that could have done without it for another couple days. It helped to occupy her mind and almost kept her from imagining Jack outside, patrolling one last time tonight.

Almost.

Of course, ignoring the routine they'd fallen into for the past two months was an impossibility. They had been worried about losing stock since the first disappearances began, nearly three months ago. The brooding fear had only escalated when apparent thefts turned into senseless mutilations and had spiked almost beyond endurance with Luke Dalton's murder and Mauricio Jurado's recent butchery.

Sonya knew that Marshal Ruggles had his hands full watching over Hades, understood his legal jurisdiction did not stretch to the protection of outlying farms, but *someone* should be doing *something* to relieve the local state of siege. With no reaction from the Pima County sheriff's office, Sonya knew Charley Shibell would not be getting Jack's vote when he ran for reelection and, while women could not vote as yet in Arizona Territory, Sonya denounced his inactivity to other local friends at any given opportunity.

Still, that was looking fourteen months into the future and a lot could change by then.

How many more people would die by then?

Thinking about Luke Dalton and Mauricio Jurado, though she'd never met or even glimpsed them to her knowledge, Sonya Conyers broke off dusting long enough to double-check the Cloverleaf revolver weighing down her apron's pocket. She did not withdraw it, knowing that its cylinder was fully loaded, but she wondered—not for the first time—if it would keep her safe against the district's unknown predator.

The Colt measured ten inches overall, counting its three-inch barrel, and it weighed just under sixteen ounces empty, four cartridges tipping its weight over one pound. Luke had advised her that its range was relatively short, suggesting that she aim dead-center at a man-sized target from no more than twenty feet and make her first shot count.

But if the target wasn't human, all of that went out the window right away.

Tiring of her busywork, Sonya drifted toward the front door of their farmhouse which was flanked by tightly-shuttered windows. Listening, her ear not quite pressed up against the door, she heard the cattle moving in their slow procession from corral to barn, where they would spend the night securely locked away.

Or as securely as her husband could arrange, at least.

Unconsciously, she slipped her hand into the apron's pocket, fingers fastening around her pistol's rounded "bird's head" grip. Her thumb rested upon the Colt's hammer but did not cock it, which would free the sensitive spur trigger from its metal sheath below the fluted cylinder.

The very last thing Sonya needed was to shoot herself by accident, maybe to bleed out on the floor while Luke was locked outside, trying to batter down the door.

Eavesdropping on the night through inch-thick wooden planks was difficult but Sonya heard the barn's door scraping shut across bare soil and pictured Jack securing the wooden beam that held it shut. That would not stop a human prowler opening the barn, of course, but from their bedroom at the northwest corner of the house, she reckoned one or both of them should hear intruders fumbling at the door, followed by lowing from the cattle they'd disturbed inside.

And from the bedroom window, once he'd flung it open, Luke could quickly bring them under fire with his Winchester.

Sonya had no fear that he would hesitate or waste a

warning shot on any creeping would-be rustlers. No one would condemn Jack if he killed in the defense of home, his family and livelihood.

In fact, if he could end the local reign of terror, Jack would be a local hero, possibly collect the cash reward that had been pledged by shopkeepers in Hades if the latest rumors were correct.

Sonya knew that her man would not return directly to the house once he'd secured the barn. It was his habit, since the troubles started, to complete a final circuit of their property and smaller outbuildings before he turned in for the night. And this night, she decided, if he was not too exhausted, Sonya planned to give him a reward.

The thought of that, a sweet anticipation, raised her somber mood and made her smile.

Jack Conyers walked around the outdoor privy, scanning shadows that the half-moon drew across his path as he completed his nightly patrol. Along the way, he almost hoped for trouble and a chance to end it, for himself, for Sonya, for their neighbors.

Not to be some kind of hero mind you, whatever that meant, but simply to resume the life they'd built together without festering under a pall of fear.

He checked the toolshed next, and passed on toward the smokehouse, his last stop before he went back to the house, knocked on the door, and slipped inside to put the night behind him. Nothing so far to arouse suspicion, nothing out of place.

But then...

A noise Conyers could not identify demanded his attention, brought him doubling back to check the barn again. This time, rounding the privy, he beheld a kind of man-shaped shadow standing at the double doors, but no man ever known to walk the Earth had ever managed to achieve this size.

Jack guessed the figure must have stood some nine feet tall, at least, and measured nearly half that width across its back and shoulders. He mistook it for a man's shadow, at first, but then discovered that there was no smaller form in front of it to cast a shade by moonlight. There was only shadow, but a murky one, almost like fog sculpted into a human's form.

And when it moved, the thing's dimensions changed before Jack's eyes.

Frozen in place with fear, Jack watched the thing reach out with taloned hands and start to lift the wooden plank that latched the barn's door. As it did, its shoulders ducked and swelled, in imitation of a man performing the appointed task, but making it seem wider and more solid than before.

Conyers had seen enough.

Raising his Winchester, he sighted quickly down the rifle's barrel, cocked its hammer with his thumb, and fired a shot precisely at the juncture where a tall man's spine would pass between his shoulder blades.

It should have been a killing shot, piercing the heart, or at the very least dropping his enemy into a heap of paralytic limbs, waiting to die in seconds as his chest filled up with blood.

Instead, the massive figure seemed to *ripple* with the .44 slug's impact. Conyers heard his bullet strike the barn's door, having no effect on his intended target, then the shadow-shape swung toward him, uttering a snarl that would have done a grizzly proud.

The thing was facing Conyers now, although he saw no features where the face should be. No, strike that. There were eyes, or something like them, but unrecognizable as human. They were flickering a dim red light as if someone had torn holes in a curtain to reveal a pair of candles burning on the other side.

Jack froze, his muscles feeling petrified. That spell was only broken when the shadow thing began advancing toward him, long legs eating up the space between them. Jack found that he could move then, pumping the Winchester's lever action rapidly and triggering shot after shot at virtually point-blank range. He was not *missing* but his slugs had no effect on his dark enemy. With each hit, Jack beheld a kind of tremor, like a small stone dropped onto the surface of a rock quarry's deep pond. Each hit evoked another snark and, when the rifle's hammer fell onto an empty chamber, Conyers swung the Yellow Boy, using its stock to club his foe across the face.

Instead, it passed straight through the oval meant to be a skull, leaving a wispy trail behind as if disturbing long black hair. Jack felt resistance, for a heartbeat, but no jolt of impact that should have resulted from the rifle striking flesh and bone.

He dropped the rifle, drew his Schofield from its holster, cursing as the night thing reached for him. Its hands, the size of Sonya's skillet, gripped Jack's upper arms with strength enough to stop their circulation almost instantly. Conyers still managed to unload the six-gun, rapid-firing it into the monster's chest before the empty weapon tumbled from his tingling hand.

All six shots wasted as if fired into a bale of hay.

The creature shook him, rattling Jack's brain inside his skull but Dalton still heard Sonya calling out his name. She'd left the house in answer to his gunfire, despite his orders to remain safely inside.

She shouted, "Let him go!" and trailed the order with obscenities that she had never uttered in Jack's presence, even in the throes of passion. Fury radiated from her voice before she raised her Colt and opened fire.

The first two shots missed Conyers, then her third drilled through his left thigh, causing him to gasp in pain. A fourth shot also missed him, may have struck the shadow giant, but Jack could not tell.

As Sonya fired her last shot from the Cloverleaf, the creature spread its hands, still clutching Jack's biceps, and twisted as it ripped his arms out of their sockets. Conyers screamed, a barely human noise, and tumbled to the ground, blood spurting from his severed shoulder stumps. Somewhere behind him, as he writhed and twisted on the sod, he heard a shriek from Sonya, indicating that she'd seen him being severed, limb from limb.

How long could he survive with that traumatic double amputation? Minutes? Maybe only seconds longer?

Before his dying mind could wrap itself around the concept of his own demise, Jack's killer raised one of its giant feet and brought it down atop his heaving abdomen. Titanic weight compressed his rib cage, then passed *through* it, as if he were made of tissue paper, grinding his internal organs into pulp. His heart and lungs went last, bursting like ripe tomatoes in a grocer's press, filling Jack's throat and mouth with hot, fresh blood.

It could be argued that his brain was dead before the monster reached his widow, lifting her with one hand tangled in her auburn hair, the other thrust beneath her long skirt, but Jack's face was turned in that direction nonetheless, mouth yawing in a final cry of pain and grief before relief and darkness settled over him at last.

FIVE

HADES: SEPTEMBER 7, 1877

Gideon Thorn was waiting when O'Grady's restaurant opened for breakfast service on the stroke of 6:00 a.m. A short brunette waitress brightened his morning with a smile and showed him to a window table facing Easy Street, leaving a menu with him as she left to fetch a mug of coffee.

Breakfast offerings were listed on the menu's left-hand page once Thorn had opened it. He scanned them quickly, opting for the corned beef hash topped with a scrambled egg, plus breaded mushrooms, and a pile of fried potatoes on the side. Toast rounded out his order, and he sipped the strong black coffee while he eyed the street outside, watching the small town wake up to another Friday morning.

What would this day bring?

More questioning of locals, after breakfast, unless Marshal Ruggles found Thorn first and they departed on the promised tour of outlying crime scenes.

In fact, Gideon's plate was barely clean when he spied Ruggles crossing Easy Street in the direction of O'Grady's, one hand raised to halt a mounted rider in his tracks before the horse and lawman could collide. Thorn paid his bill and left a tip, clearing the exit to meet Ruggles on the sidewalk just as he arrived.

"There's been another one," the grim-faced marshal said. "Sometime last night."

Thorn did not have to ask his meaning but he sought to amplify the information offered. "Livestock, or...?"

"People. Two victims this time. Man and wife, a Jack and Sonya Conyers. They have—or *had*—a spread southwest of town."

"Same kind of thing as with the last two victims?" Thorn inquired.

Ruggles grimaced. "Worse, from what I've heard so far. A neighbor passing spotted Jack and Sonya in the yard outside their house. Checked on the cattle in the barn but they seemed fine aside from being late for feed and water. After that, he rode straight here, shaking so bad he barely got the story out before he left to rush back home."

"Tell me," Gideon urged.

"I'd rather show you," Ruggles said, "but basically, the two of them were torn apart from what I gather. Jack had both arms torn out of their sockets and his midsection was crushed, whatever that means. Witness said it looked like 'something big' stepped on him after he was down."

"And the widow?"

"According to the neighbor, something pulled her head off, pitching it across the yard. He said her clothes were shredded but he couldn't say if anyone had...interfered with her. Ashamed to get that close, I guess, or scared out of his mind."

"You're riding out there now?" asked Gideon.

"Just came to look for you," Ruggles replied. "I've got our undertaker and his helper hitching up their wagon and our doctor standing by to give us an opinion on the bodies."

"I'll just need to get my stallion from the livery," Thorn said, "and meet you where?"

"West end of town," said Ruggles. "We'll be ready."

Before heading to the livery, Thorn doubled back to his hotel and fetched the Winchester out of his chifforobe. As ready as he'd ever be to view another slaughter site, he walked down to the stable, reaching out before he got there to alert Shadow and Belle. The hostler, Monte Rifkin was already sweeping up and hat a pot of coffee on. He greeted Thorn, offered a cup, and Gideon declined with thanks, explaining that he didn't have the time to spare.

"Bad doings at the Conyers place, I hear," Rifkin advised.

"Sounds like it."

"I don't know what Pima County's coming to, a thing like this. Ain't human, if you want to know what I think."

"Hard to say," Thorn answered back. "Some people make wild animals look tame."

"Amen to that. At least, if it's a man, we'll get to see him stretching a rope."

Thorn soothed his animals with quiet thoughts while getting Shadow saddled for the road. Belle didn't seem to mind being excluded from the road trip, satisfied to feast on oats, then settle in for a siesta in her stall. The stallion, by comparison, was keen to stretch his legs and see what new adventure lay in store. Shadow had steady nerves, was not gun-shy by any means, and he had never failed Thorn when it came to standing fast in danger's path.

Gideon followed Easy Street to where Brett Ruggles sat

astride a bay mare with white stockings on her two front legs. Beside the marshal and his mount, a wagon sat with three men on its high seat, twin black geldings harnessed up to it. The marshal introduced Thorn to the undertaker first, a gray man by the name of Arnold Primm, then to the doctor serving Hades, Julius Maddox, sandy-haired and thirty-odd years old. The middleman—or boy, more properly—was Primm's odd-job assistant, Todd Mulaney, somewhere in his latter teens.

The wagon's bed contained two plain pine boxes, ready to receive whatever might remain of Jack and Sonya Conyers after they'd been murdered overnight and left exposed to desert scavengers.

Thorn was not looking forward to the grisly scene as they rode out but long experience had taught him that he learned more from observing than from simply hearing nightmare stories told second- or third-hand.

Their trip consumed the best part of an hour with the sun already beating down on the uneasy travelers. They traveled on in silence, save for creaking from the undertaker's wagon and the *clip-clop* of their horses' hooves, each member of the party wondering and dreading what might lie in store for them upon arrival.

They saw vultures first, from half a mile away, circling above the Conyers ranch. When they had closed the distance to one hundred yards, Thorn saw that a fair number of the birds, drawn to a feast of carrion, had settled in the farmyard and along the roof of what must now be an abandoned house. At fifty yards, they heard the rancher's pent-up cattle lowing, calling from release from the barn where they'd spent a restless night.

Thorn saw the marshal draw his sidearm and was ready for the gunshot Ruggles triggered when they'd closed to thirty yards. Its echo sent the buzzards flapping skyward, squawking protests over the disturbance of their breakfast feast. It also further agitated the cattle trapped inside the barn but Ruggles focused first on what remained of Jack and Sonya Conyers, littering the farmyard between its unoccupied corral and the small house whose front door stood ajar.

The corpses, what remained of them, were not the worst that Gideon had seen but they came close. A softly muttered, "Jesus God!" from Dr. Maddox fairly summarized the situation and Thorn noted Todd Mulaney gnawing on his lower lip as he surveyed the carnage spread before them.

Jack Conyers was lying supine, face turned toward the unrelenting sun, eyes open to its glare, already faded to the hue of milky marbles. Both arms had been wrenched out of their sockets by some means unknown, each separated from the rancher's torso by a good six feet or more.

Torn off and tossed aside, Gideon thought, trying to picture who or what had managed to accomplish that. A bear could rip a man's arm off, of course, but it would need to tackle one before the other. Thorn doubted that even an adult grizzly—if the species still survived in Arizona Territory—would waste time removing *both* arms without eating either one.

And then, there was the crushing wound inflicted somehow on the rancher's abdomen, as if some creature of prodigious size and weight had trodden on his chest—but only once, in passing, without opening the body for a meal of organ meat.

Thorn sent a calming thought to Shadow while dismounting, joined by Ruggles as they scanned the grisly scene. Doc Maddox seemed reluctant to step down from

Arnold Primm's wagon but recognized that he had work to do, even if he'd arrived too late to be of any use. The undertaker and his sidekick both stayed seated, waiting for the marshal and the doctor to finish examining the scene.

Both took their time surveying Jack Conyers, agreeing that a first look gave no clue to who or what had been responsible for killing him. They ruled out bear and cougar, before Maddox asked, "You notice something, Marshal?"

Ruggles crouched beside the sundered corpse, face twisted up against the smell, and finally replied, "Nothing's been at him. Fresh meat should have brought coyotes, maybe even javelinas, but there's no sign I can see that anything's been feeding on him overnight."

"Or since then," Dr. Maddox said. "It's broad daylight. Do you see any flies buzzing around?"

Thorn hadn't noted that discrepancy but caught it now. Two corpses left exposed for hours should have been aswarm with insects—ants, beetles, and flies—but none such were in evidence. A full examination back in town would be required but Gideon imagined it would fail to turn up any creeping things.

And what did *that* mean?

Aside from the removal of both arms and the implosion of his rib cage, Jack Conyers had suffered no other apparent major injuries.

The same could not be said about his wife.

If Jack Conyers was partially dismembered, with his viscera compressed, wife Sonya had been torn apart as if during a tug of war between wild beasts. Her head, apparently removed by twisting of her neck, lay midway in between her body and her former home's front porch, face down in the dust and screened by hair clotted with blood. When Dr. Maddox nudged the head onto its side,

Thorn glimpsed its facial features frozen in a silent scream.

Of her original four limbs, Sonya had only one—the left arm—still connected to her body, and that arm was broken at the elbow, angled and inverted so the palm of her left hand was pointed skyward, fingers curled into it like the legs of a dead spider. Her right arm and both legs had been wrenched away and scattered, while her homespun dress was ripped open from collar down to hem, flung back to place her pitiful remains on full display.

In other circumstances, Thorn might have pronounced the damage a demented sex crime but the injuries he saw were all intended to dismantle Sonya, none of them to penetrate lasciviously.

Gideon stood back, leaving the lawman and physician to complete their first examination of the victims. Finally, Ruggles asked him, "Have you seen anything like this before?"

"Not even close," Thorn answered back. "This doesn't look like animals to me."

"What, then?"

Gideon shrugged. "Beats me. I had a case with cannibals a while back, in Missouri..."

"Christ, don't tell me that," Ruggles protested.

"It was nothing like this," Thorn assured him. "That bunch killed to feed, like wolves. They wouldn't leave a meal behind."

Todd Mulaney jumped down from the wagon seat and ran around behind it, doubling over out of sight as he expelled his breakfast. His companions, understanding, took care not to notice his embarrassment, though August Primm handed a canteen to his young associate.

"All right," the marshal said at last. "We'd better get

them loaded up and back to town. Maybe the doc can find something we've overlooked."

"It's possible," Maddox agreed, "but nothing much is hidden from us here. Don't hold out any hope for knife or gunshot wounds under Jack's clothes. And Sonya, well..."

"We have to try, at least," said Ruggles. "I'll owe Charley Shibell a report, whether he bothers reading it or not."

The undertaker called out to Mulaney, "Are you good there, Todd?"

"Good as I'll ever be again," the teen replied.

"Let's get them in the caskets, then," Primm ordered, scrambling from the wagon as if he confronted scenes like this one every day.

More racket from the barn distracted Thorn and Ruggles from the team transferring the remains of Jack and Sonya Conyers into separate pine boxes, crudely reassembling each of them before the lids were set in place.

"We'd better see about the animals," Ruggles allowed. "Make sure they're all intact, at least."

"If they've been cooped up in the barn all night, they might appreciate some time in the corral," Thorn said.

"With feed and water," Ruggles said. "If we can manage that, I'll need to have a word with Ernie Fletcher. See if he can care for them, or maybe even take them home, while I try running down some next of kin."

"Jack told me once he had a sister in Louisiana somewhere," Dr. Maddox offered, "but I don't recall her married name off-hand."

"Worse comes to worst, I'll hand them over to the county."

Frowning, Maddox answered, "I'd have said that worse already came to worst."

"You any good with stock?" Ruggles asked Gideon.

"I'll do my best."

He opened the corral's gate first, then mounted Shadow while the marshal drew his six-gun and approached the barn. Ruggles was cautious, opening the double doors, but then a hefty bull brushed past him, on a beeline for its normal outdoor pen, the other cattle trailing it in fair approximation of a pastoral parade. Gideon counted thirty head all told, trooping past Shadow without giving Thorn or his stallion a second glance.

Both mutilated bodies had been stowed in pine as Thorn and Ruggles started hauling feed to the corral, then going to the outdoor well and drawing water for the nearly-empty trough. When it was brimming full, Ruggles fastened the gate and walked back to his mare.

"I reckon that's the best that we can do for now," he said. "I need to speak with Ernie Fletcher next, before I head back into town. You want to come along, Gideon? Find out what he has to say?"

"Seems like the next logical step. He needs formal elimination as a suspect, anyway."

"Suspect for *this*?" Ruggles made no attempt to mask his incredulity. "I've known him and his family for five, six years, at least. I don't believe he's capable of anything like this."

"And there's no reason to believe you're wrong," Gideon said. "But sometimes people who report a crime are tied into it somehow. I'd prefer to get a feel for that from Mr. Fletcher, face to face."

"Okay, then. You're the expert," Ruggles granted.

"Not with anything like this," Thorn said. And thought, *Not yet at least.*

With feed and water readily available, the Conyers cattle did not seem to miss their former owners. Gideon and Ruggles watched the undertaker's wagon rolling back toward Hades with its grim cargo before the marshal set a course for Ernie Fletcher's spread and Thorn fell into place at his right hand.

Concealed in long, dry grass, a native tribesman watched the whites depart and separate, unnoticed as the mounted riders passed him at a range of thirty yards. Beside the slender gray-haired watcher, warmed by desert sunshine, lay a single-shot Sharps carbine popular with cavalry of both contending armies in the U.S. Civil War, recovered from a smoky battlefield located at Picacho Pass, northwest of Tucson, in mid-April 1862.

The watcher did not plan to fire upon the riders passing by, though he was of a mind to follow them and find out where they went after collecting corpses from the Conyers ranch. He had arrived on site before the visitors from Hades, recognized the evidence of what had happened overnight, and now was forced to choose what he should do about it, whether intervening or remaining an observer as events continued to unfold.

That choice would not come easily and, if the watcher chose to interfere, he would need better weapons than a scrap of iron and wood designed for slaying mortal men.

The old man's name was Hania, translated from his native Yaquis tongue to "spirit warrior" in the white man's English or, to Spanish, as *guerrero spiritual.* He had been appointed as a shaman at the age of nineteen summers but, of late, had fallen out of favor with some younger members of his tribe. Ignored and sometimes ridiculed, Hania held his tongue, refrained from offering opinions where they were not wanted but was still a prescient observer of events that might affect his people and their ultimate survival over time.

Hania's unshod Appaloosa pony was concealed some fifty yards behind him, cropping grass within a desert gully, well below the land's skyline. He waited for the two white riders to recede, then rose and jogged back to the dry wash, mounted up, and set off in a slow, cautious pursuit of them. They would not see him if he kept his distance, something every Yaqui learned around the age when he or she began to walk.

Hania rode bareback with a plain rope halter, and urged his pony from the gully with brief pressure from his moccasins. He held the carbine loosely, propped across his lap, but had no thought of using it today.

The white men he was trailing might not be his enemies in spirit and the creature he was hunting now, daily, was impervious to rifle fire.

Which did not mean it was immortal, not by any means.

The lawman out of Hades could not help Hania, either, but the man in black who rode beside him...well, he had a certain aura that might prove more useful in the conflict yet to come.

That is, if the stranger and Hania could agree on certain terms.

But with the gulf of history and race lying between them, could that ever come to pass?

After a mile or so, the old man knew where Marshal Ruggles and his friend in black were going. Although personally unacquainted with them, Hania kept tabs on all the local settlers who had occupied his peoples' former hunting grounds over the years. He knew their names, the number of their offspring, when they celebrated marriages and mourned the loss of loved ones. More of them were grieving now than in years past, though no fault of Hania's, he knew the man responsible.

But could he stop it, even with assistance from the man dressed all in black?

And if he *did,* would that be counted as betrayal of his brothers who had lost so much already to the territory's miners, ranchers, and homesteaders? Who among his kinsmen would be grateful for Hania's intervention? Which would curse his name?

And in the end, would he even survive?

That hardly mattered now. Hania had already set his course of action, knew what must be done to help restore natural order in his world. The fate of one old man would make no difference and, while he felt no pressing urge to die, he owed the effort to his ancestors, the children of Yomumuli, the first hunter, who had thrown fire at the sun and water at the moon before the Spaniards came and decimated native people everywhere.

Where a god had failed to halt that cruel invasion and the waves that followed, Hania knew why a remnant of his people, even now, might seek to stem the tide but they were doomed to fail while opening the door to ancient evil from Beyond.

The old man would die trying to prevent that if he could but knew that he could not succeed alone.

SIX

The Fletcher place was nothing special at a glance but Thorn could recognize the work that had gone into it, raising a house and barn, with smaller outbuildings, and managing to cultivate a meager field of crops from arid desert soil. That took determination and life teetered on a knife's edge from one season to the next with nothing guaranteed but more hard labor without end.

As they approached the homestead, Marshal Ruggles treated Thorn to sketchy background on the farmer and his family.

"Ernie Fletcher and his wife, Clarice, keep this place going with their boys, Vincent and Matt," he said. "Unlike most others hereabouts, they scratch a living from the ground instead of putting all their money into livestock. Irrigation's from a string of wells that Ernie's excavated over time. They do all right, I guess, selling whatever surplus they compile, and raise some hogs for meat. Sometimes their pork is on the menu at O'Grady's and Casa del Sol, in town."

"No easy life," Gideon mused.

"They make it work somehow," the marshal said. "Or did, at least, until this trouble came along. I'd guess they're having second thoughts right now."

"Will they be expecting visitors?" Thorn asked.

"Should be. I told Ernie we'd need to have more words after he tipped me off this morning."

"So, no random shooting, then?"

"Let's hope not," Ruggles said.

Thorn did not reach down for his Winchester, leery of starting trouble, but he did release the hammer thong that held his right-hand Colt securely in its holster. Beyond that, he'd have to trust the marshal and his knowledge of the individuals who'd planted homesteads in the desert that surrounded Hades.

They found Ernie Fletcher waiting for them on his porch. Thorn didn't know the man from Adam but he took his cue from Ruggles calling out as they approached, and Fletcher raised one hand in a silent greeting. In the open doorway just behind him, Gideon made out a woman watching, flanked by two boys clinging to her gingham skirt.

"Who's this, then?" Fletcher asked the marshal, eyeing Thorn as his two visitors reined in before the farmhouse.

"Friend of mine," Ruggles replied, perhaps exaggerating. "He's had some experience with things like this."

"Friend got a name?" the farmer asked.

"I do," Gideon answered, followed with his name, and let it go at that. Unlike his first reception at the *Hades Flame,* it obviously failed to ring a bell in Ernie Fletcher's mind.

"Experience with 'things like this' you say, Marshal?" Fletcher made no attempt to mask his skepticism as he kept his eyes on Thorn.

"Nothing *exactly* like it," Gideon corrected. "I look into

strange events from time to time and see what I can make of them."

"That's how you make a living?" Ernie asked him.

"More or less," said Gideon refusing to be drawn into discussion of his economic status.

"And you put things right?" the farmer pressed.

"More times than not," Thorn answered back. "No guarantees, of course."

"Sounds like the story of our lives out here," Fletcher replied and spat into the farmyard's dust.

Ruggles apparently decided it was time to end the fencing match. "We've just come from the Conyers place," he told Fletcher. "They're headed into town with August Primm right now."

"What's left of 'em," Fletcher amended.

"Any chance that we can talk about this in the shade?" Ruggles inquired.

"I reckon so," their host replied. "Tie up and come on in."

The house looked smaller from the outside than it did once they were standing in the combination living room and kitchen. Riding up, it had looked boxy, almost square, but now Thorn saw two bedrooms that extended eastward, hidden as they closed the distance on their first approach.

"Got coffee on," Fletcher advised, "you wanna take a load off at the table. It's too early to be feeding you."

"Coffee's perfect," Ruggles agreed, doffing his hat before he sat down at the hand-hewn dining table, careful not to take the head seat that belonged to Ernie Fletcher as the lord and master of his spread.

Thorn took his cue from Ruggles, slipped his hat off, ready for it when the farmer's wife and sons gaped at the white streak running down the middle of his scalp from hairline to the crown. The older boy seemed on the point of asking Thorn about it when his mother intervened, telling her sons, "Get in your room right now."

The Fletcher boys departed, grumbling, the adults remaining silent till their bedroom door had been securely shut. Once that was done, Brett Ruggles spoke, keeping his voice pitched low.

"Ernie, first thing, I want to thank you for your tip this morning. What you found is legally outside my jurisdiction as town marshal but I'm hoping it may bring some action from the sheriff's office."

Ernie Fletcher made a kind of snorting noise. Said, "Hope in one hand, Marshal, while you're spitting in the other. See which fills up first."

"Sheriff Shibell's got no friends hereabouts," Clarice Fletcher chimed in. "I'm only sorry that he's got another three years on the job."

Ruggles nodded. Replied, "I hear you but I have to run this latest information past him, all the same. Assuming he does nothing with it—"

"That's a safe assumption," Ernie Fletcher interjected.

Ruggles frowned, then forged ahead. "I'll see what Mr. Thorn and I can do to stop these raids."

Fletcher half turned to face Thorn more directly, saying, "I'm not clear on who you are or what it is you do."

"Long story short," said Gideon, "when I was two years old, a creature from the Rockies up in Colorado—Kansas Territory in those days—attacked my family, killing my parents and my older brother. I survived with this—" he passed a hand over the white blaze on his scalp —"but never lost my need to know what was responsible."

"Sounds like a grizzly," Ernie Fletcher said.

"That was the popular opinion when our sheriff swept it underneath the rug," Thorn said.

"And that has a familiar ring to it," Clarice remarked.

"Jumping a few years forward," Thorn continued, "I got lucky with a relative in Boston that I never heard of, growing up. She educated me, then passed away shortly before I was supposed to enter law school. Since then, I've been applying my inheritance to traveling and solving mysteries while hoping I could catch up with the thing that changed my life."

"And did you, ever?" Ernie Fletcher asked him.

"Ernest, honestly!" his wife half-whispered.

"No, ma'am, that's all right," Thorn said. "I did, in fact, last summer when the killings started up again. It's dead now, not to say there aren't more like it, hiding out somewhere. Be that as it may, investigating secrets, trying to find answers and save lives along the way...I guess you'd say it's grown into a habit that I can't let go."

Frowning, the farmer asked, "And have you run across a thing like we've been living with?"

"No, this is new," said Gideon. "All I can promise you is that I'll do my very best to stop it, if I can."

"All well and good," Fletcher replied as he began to roll himself a cigarette. "But I supposed the marshal here has told you my whole part in it. I had some early shopping planned in Hades, then I spotted buzzards all around the Conyers place and found what you already say. High-tailed it into town and then back home, praying I'd find my wife and young-uns safe."

"And nothing more you could have done," Ruggles opined.

"I second that," Thorn said. "My only question would be whether you've remembered any little thing at all that might have slipped your mind in the excitement, talking to the marshal."

"Any little thing like what?" the farmer asked around a puff of tart tobacco smoke.

"I can't begin to guess," Gideon said. "A first impression, possibly, like the suggestion of a footprint, maybe more than one, before the sun got any higher and brought on a morning wind?"

Fletcher considered that and shook his head. "Sorry. Nothing like that. With Jack and Sonya lying in the yard like that, all tore to pieces, tracks and such were just about the last thing on my mind."

"What were the vultures doing when you got there?" Gideon inquired.

"Doing? Just sizing up their breakfast, I suppose."

"I mean, were any of them feeding?" Thorn elaborated.

"Not when I rode up," Fletcher replied. "Reckon I spooked them."

Gideon glanced over toward the marshal, saw that he was thinking of what they'd observed on visiting the Conyers ranch. No insects or nocturnal scavengers had touched the corpses, giving them a wide berth in clear violation of the desert's dining etiquette. Even the vultures, who were plentiful, had kept their distance from the mutilated bodies as if watching over them in lieu of feasting while they had the chance.

Almost as if they deemed the torn remains to be unclean.

"Okay, then," Gideon advised. "That's all the questions I can think of at the moment."

He donned his hat as Ruggles rose to leave and thanked the Fletchers for their time. "Whoever or whatever's doing this," the lawman said, "there's been no raid against crop farmers yet, but I don't have to tell you to be extra-careful."

"No, you don't Marshal," Ernie replied. "I take care of my own the very best I can."

"And that's all anyone can do right now," Ruggles replied.

Outside, late-morning desert heat struck Gideon with all the impact of a slap across the face. He mounted Shadow, tipped his hat to Ernie and his wife as Ruggles settled on his bay mare, and the two of them turned back toward town.

Toward Hades, on a day that promised to be hot as hell.

Hania watched the riders leave, concealed within a copse of trees three hundred yards distant from the farmhouse they had been visiting. They started back toward town but he delayed departure from his hideout, letting them pass out of sight and waiting to discover if the farmer or his family would soon emerge.

When no one left the house after ten minutes, counted silently inside the old man's head, he mounted up and made tracks eastward, toward the latest now-abandoned murder ranch. He needed time to take a closer look around, uninterrupted, and to think about the best way to contact the man in black.

Entering Hades on his own in broad daylight would be a terrible idea. White occupants of Hades were uneasy around Native tribesmen at the best of times, much less when they were being slaughtered by some unknown force they could not understand. Hania knew he'd have a better chance of getting in and out alive once night fell on the desert but he'd still have to locate the man in black, catch him alone, and hope that he might listen to an old red man whom he's never met before.

There was no mystery involved in where the stranger would be lodging since the town had only one hotel. No Yaqui would be welcomed on the premises but Hania was reasonably sure that he could watch and wait—all night, if need be—for an opportunity, however brief, to state his case.

And something told him that the man in black was wise enough to listen, possibly to act and help Hania end the nightmare that had settled over southern Pima County.

That, of course, would also mean facing Hania's enemies within the Yaqui tribe and very possibly inviting his own death.

So be it, he decided.

There were times in life when it was best to watch and wait, others when action was required. And what did any old man's life matter with so much riding on the line?

Hania had a duty to his people, to his ancestors and the Great Spirits, to forestall creation from being corrupted and uprooted if he had the power to prevent it. And if he should fail...well, at the very least he would have done his best.

There was a certain irony to seeking out a white man for assistance in that struggle but Hania recognized when he could not perform a task all on his own. If only he had picked the *right* outsider to collaborate with him.

Confirming that required a private interview if that proved feasible.

If not, the old man knew he must proceed alone, asking Yomumuli and Itom Ae, the Earth Mother, for strength to purge the plague of darkness that had fallen over Pima County.

Failing that, Hania reckoned that his mission would have failed and that he would have lost his soul.

HADES

Once they were back in town, the marshal went to check with Dr. Maddox and find out if he'd learned any more about the Conyers couple and their cause of death. Gideon Thorn, despite all he had seen that morning, still felt pangs of hunger after he'd stowed Shadow at the livery and walked down to procure lunch from Casa del Sol.

The restaurant was nearly full this noontime but the hostess led Thorn to a small table for two located near the kitchen. The aromas wafting through its batwing doors enticed him as he scanned he ordered beer, then scanned the menu while he waited for the foamy mug to reach him.

In his travels, Thorn had seen most any kind of damage that a beast or man could manage to inflict on human beings. New things, like the carnage he had witnessed on the Conyers' spread that morning, still surprised him but it rarely jarred him as it had when he was still new to investigations of the unexplained.

If that meant he was jaded, Gideon supposed that he would have to live with it and forge ahead in his pursuit of natural—and some *un*natural—anomalies.

He wound up ordering a *chimichanga*—shredded beef and chicken in a fried burrito—with an enchilada and tamale, rice and refried beans, plus freshly-made tortillas that would let him swab his plate to keep from missing anything. The food, when it arrived, was plentiful and spiced with chile peppers that encouraged Thorn to have a second beer and cool his palate as he finished up.

Thorn took his time over the meal, in no great rush to hear the doctor's verdict as relayed to Marshal Ruggles. He had seen the damage for himself and knew already that it mimicked nothing he had seen before, during long years of finding bodies drowned, shot, partially devoured or swallowed whole, some drained of blood but otherwise intact—the list went on until Thorn put it out of mind and finished mopping up his nearly-clean plate with the last of his tortillas, chasing it with beer.

"All good here, sir?" the waitress asked as she swung by his corner table.

"Perfect," Gideon replied although he'd never felt at ease when someone called him "sir."

"So glad to hear it. Any room left for dessert? The chef's made flan today and if you've never tried it—"

"Wish I could," Thorn answered with a smile. "But I still have to make it back to the hotel."

She laughed at that and left his check. It added up and Thorn tacked on an extra dollar for the grins and repartee, leaving Casa del Sol before the waitress had a chance to thank him one more time.

Outside, with early afternoon advancing, Thorn saw Ruggles moving toward him, nodding as he passed townsfolk, replying to the questions that bombarded him but never fully breaking stride.

As he approached, the marshal said, "I tried O'Grady's first, then had to run a gauntlet as you see."

"I like to switch it up," Gideon said. "Thought I might have a quick drink at The Prairie Dog before I tried to track you down."

"Sounds good," the lawman said. "I'll tag along."

"Any surprises from the doctor or the undertaker?" Thorn inquired, as they moved on.

"Nothing that wasn't obvious this morning," Ruggles answered. "Neither one of them can figure why the bugs and buzzards passed on chowing down."

"Is there an estimate on time of death?"

"Doc Maddox says sometime around midnight but, with the damage, it's a guessing game. There should have been coyotes out and who knows what all before sunrise brought the vultures in."

"Almost like something warned them off," said Gideon.

"Something like what?"

"Wish I could help you there, Marshal, but I'm drawing a blank." Approaching the saloon, he asked, "Was it the same way with the other bodies or the livestock?"

"Truth be told, nobody thought to check. They're in the ground now—the two men, that is—and bonfires took the animals."

"No way of knowing whether it's a pattern, then," Thorn said.

"I like this less the more I see of it," Ruggles replied.

"That's understandable. When you start getting used to things, it's time to worry."

"God forbid that happens here."

They'd reached The Prairie Dog and paused outside its double swinging doors. "I can't predict what happens next," said Thorn, "but come what may, I'm not convinced God had a lot to do with it."

"Some folks are saying it's the Devil," Ruggles said, frowning. "Blaming whoever named Hades in the first place, like it was some kind of invitation."

"I can't speak to that," Gideon said. "I guess your preachers got a few ideas about it, though."

"Reverend Connor Blake at Mercy Baptist," Ruggles answered, nodding. "He didn't draw much of a crowd on Sundays prior to June but, now, he packs them in. Hey, you don't think he might be...?"

"Doubtful," Thorn replied, "considering the injuries we saw today, but anyone's worth looking at until we have a better lead."

"I'll have a word with him. Soft-pedal it for now. He's only five-foot-two or-three. Can't see him managing all that's been done so far unless he had a gang to help him."

"Mind if I talk to him myself?" Thorn asked. "Just introduce myself and get his take on what's been happening?"

"Okay by me," Ruggles replied. "I should advise you, though, that Blake's a fire and brimstone kind of guy. These killings are the biggest news to hit Hades since I've been marshaling. One way to look at it, they're all that's kept his church alive this summer."

Gideon refrained from mentioning the obvious—that a full house on Sundays and the income it provided for the local sky pilot might constitute a motive—waiting to reserve judgment until he met the minister himself.

"I'll head down once we've had that drink, then," he told Ruggles. "Nothing pushy, just an interested stranger passing through."

"You might not want to mention we're cooperating on it," Ruggles said, "although it won't take long for word to get around."

They pushed into The Prairie Dog, Thorn on the marshal's heels, just as a slump-shouldered pianist in his forties started banging out "The Lost Chord," an ironic choice considering his mediocre skill and the poor tuning of his instrument.

SEVEN

One drink turned into three but Thorn was clear-headed and steady on his feet when they departed from The Prairie Dog and went their separate ways. Ruggles was on his way to telegraph the Pima County sheriff's office in Tucson, expecting little for the effort, while Thorn ambled down to Mercy Baptist Church.

His first thought was that God's house could have used a fresh paint job but that seemed true of nearly all the shops and offices in Hades. No one on a budget could prevent the desert sun from parching wood, making its painted colors fade and peel. Given the small town's population and the relative infrequency of strangers passing through, maintenance did not seem to rate a high priority.

Thorn spent a moment standing in the shade of Mercy Baptist's steeple, pondering how he should best approach its minister. His background in religion was eclectic, leavened with his Aunt Drusilla's fascination with Spiritualism, while Obi Magoro had shared legends from West African paganism in addition to certain native martial arts. No church-goer, Thorn covered all his bets with amulets strung on a silver chain around his neck: a crucifix, a Star of David, and a crescent symbolizing Islam, plus a pagan pentagram and feather symbolizing the beliefs of tribes native to North America.

So far, none of the icons had proved useful in protecting Thorn from contact with the great unknown but there might always be a first time, somewhere down the road.

Gideon mounted creaky wooden steps and tried the front door of the church, found it unlocked, and eased his way inside. The narthex was a small room, twelve by twelve, if that, with no doors barring access to the nave beyond. Thorn counted fifteen rows of rough-hewn pews, divided by a central aisle, standing between the nave's entrance and the sanctuary, where an elevated pulpit stood, a bulky open Bible topping its presenter's shelf.

A moment passed, with no sign of the minister, before a gruff voice from behind Thorn made him turn back toward the narthex and the street beyond it.

"May I help you?"

Marshal Ruggles had been right about the preacher. He was short, stoop-shouldered, gray hair thinning on his scalp. A pair of wire-rimmed spectacles perched on his outsized nose, their lenses magnifying watery blue eyes beneath thick, bristling brows shot through with streaks of white. His suit was much like Thorn's, minus Gideon's weapons, and a gray bowtie peeked from below the sagging turkey wattle of his neck.

On balance, not a strong man, certainly not one who could dismember three armed men and one woman without substantial aid from larger, stronger cohorts.

Thorn introduced himself and Connor Blake reciprocated without offering a hand to shake. Instead, he asked, "What brings you into God's house, bearing guns?"

"I didn't see a place to check them when I walked in off the street," Gideon said.

Blake grunted in reply, as if clearing his throat, and tried another angle of attack. "The purpose of your visit?"

Thorn had pondered that and finally decided that it couldn't hurt to use the marshal's name. "I'm working with Brett Ruggles on the killings that your county has been suffering of late."

"Officially? I don't see any badge of office," Blake observed. "Are you a sheriff's deputy?"

"No, sir."

"We have no territorial police. A mercenary Pinkerton, perhaps?"

"Strictly a private citizen," Thorn said.

"And being subsidized by whom, if I may ask."

"You may," Gideon answered back. "I make my own way in the world."

"Investigating murders on a whim?"

"Your marshal doesn't seem to mind the help," Gideon parried. "Why should you?"

Blake rolled his shoulders in what might have been a listless shrug. "A time like this, a stranger comes to town. It may seem odd to some. Even suspicious, one might say."

"I've had some prior experience with cases that resisted simple answers, Reverend."

"And solved them?"

"Some."

"With what result?"

"Depends on who turned out to be responsible."

"Or *what,* perhaps?"

"That, too," Thorn granted. "Are you leaning toward a spiritual explanation for what's happening?"

"I place my trust in God," Blake said. "He will provide."

"Four settlers dead so far, livestock on top of that."

"Did you say *four*?"

It seemed to Thorn that Blake's face paled a bit as he retreated half a pace from Gideon.

"Jack Conyers and his wife, last night sometime," Thorn said. "You hadn't heard?"

"Good Lord," Baker exhaled, shaking his head. "I see a demon's hand at work here. Possibly Satan himself." Eyes narrowing, he faced Thorn. Said, "Perhaps you think that's just an old man's superstition, playing to his congregation?"

"I try not to judge before the evidence is in," Gideon answered.

"And meanwhile, people keep on dying."

"Every day. Around the world."

"May I ask *how* the latest victims were dispatched?"

"You'd best direct that question to the marshal or to Dr. Maddow," Thorn replied. "It's not my tale to tell."

That brought a frown to Baker's face. "You'd keep it from me? From the townspeople of Hades?"

"When the leaders of the town have something to announce," Thorn said, "I'm sure you'll read it in the newspaper."

"That Ellis Flynn! I don't consider him a man of God."

Thorn saw that he was getting nowhere with the minister and didn't feel like being sidetracked into character assassinations based on dogma. "I'll leave that between the two of you," he said, grazing his hat's brim with a trigger finger, "and I'll thank you for your time."

"Come back on Sunday," Baker told Thorn's back as he retreated. "This new horror will be mentioned in my sermon."

Whether you have any facts to back it up or not, Gideon

thought, as he left Mercy Baptist, stepping into bright daylight on Easy Street.

Hania stood in a shaded alley's mouth between the barbershop and Diamond Lil's Saloon, remaining out of sight from random passersby. The old Yaqui knew he was free to enter Hades, could do business at a couple of the stores if he had cash in hand, but otherwise would be unwelcome as a visitor.

The sale of alcohol, for instance, was denied to Native tribesmen throughout Arizona Territory and beyond, although the old laws banning firearms had been undercut by various amendments that pertained to hunting and to self-defense. An incident that left a white man dead might still result in lynching, even under utmost provocation, but Hania understood that matters were improving slowly—*very* slowly—for red men in the American southwest.

So far, there were four so-called reservations located in Arizona Territory. One, the oldest, founded eighteen years ago, lay along the Gila River, home to Maricopa and Pima Natives. Since 1865, the Colorado River Reservation had extended into California, housing Chemehuevi, Hopi, Mohave, and Navajo. A third, restricted to Navajos, spanned the border between Arizona and New Mexico Territories, established in 1868. Hania's ostensible homeland, the San Carlos Apache Reservation, was only five years old, and now, unknown to white authorities in Phoenix or in Washington, D.C., threatened the whole Southwest with ruin unless someone joined Hania to purge the threat.

And now, the Yaqui gray-hair saw the white man he had

earmarked as an ally in that effort drawing closer, striding down the other side of Easy Street.

Hania had seen him duck into the church, assuming that he had consulted with the praying parson who presided there. The preacher, Blake by name, despised all Natives of the continent as heathens, even those who had relinquished their traditional beliefs to grovel at the mission shrines devoted to a long-dead being whom the Spanish *padres* knew as *Jesucristo*.

Hania personally had no use for foreign gods, always depicted in religious works of art as white men graced with flowing hair and beards. If he had been presented with a book of maps, Hania could not have found the distant "Holy Land" where Anglo settlers and the *Mexicanos* they had dispossessed along with red men traced the roots of a religion that sometimes divided them and set them at each other's throats.

None of that mattered to him now, as something older, *darker*, cast a pall across the land.

The man in black was clearly bound for his hotel, the Continental. Hania had already seen him dine, then meet the town's lawman and stop for beer or whisky at The Prairie Dog before they parted company, the marshal moving toward the doctor's office while the new arrival went to church.

He had not gone to pray, Hania was reasonably sure of that. But being thorough, he would seek the shaman of Hades, perhaps solicit his opinion on the bloodshed that had scourged that part of Pima County for the past three moons. Whether he'd found a partial answer there, Hania could not say, but the expression on the white man's face showed him to be dissatisfied.

He had not found the answer he was seeking yet.

But would he listen to an old Yaqui regarded even by some members of his tribe as *loco*?

Maybe. Maybe not.

Hania could but try and that he meant to do before the day was out.

Which meant a meeting with the stranger where they would be safe from prying eyes.

Gideon Thorn entered the Continental Hotel's lobby, stopping off at the reception desk to check for any messages. He had expected none and that was what awaited him.

Climbing the stairs, he thought once more about responding to the letter he'd received from Dinah Pilcher. Thorn was not prepared to summon her from Boston to the Arizona Territory, when he couldn't say how long he'd be involved there, what he might be facing, even whether he would make it out alive.

Later, he thought, *when things calmed down*. There would be time enough to write her then, apologize for his delay in answering her message, and explaining why he had not seized the opportunity for a reunion in the West.

But would she understand? Forgive him? How much had Dinah changed during her journey of recovery from their last outing as a team?

Arriving on the second floor, Gideon stopped dead in his tracks. A man was standing in the hallway, just outside his door—not facing it as it if attempting to break in, but rather waiting patiently, watching the landing as Thorn finished his ascent.

First thing, Thorn checked the man for weapons and

saw nothing obvious beyond a hunting knife sheathed on his hip. With close to thirty feet between them, there was no way he could draw the blade and hope to use it, even if he were accomplished as a knife-thrower, before a slug from one of Thorn's Colts brought him down.

Gideon's next impression was of age, with shoulder-length gray hair but smooth, clean cheeks. That combination and the stranger's style of dress identified him as a Native tribesman, although Thorn could not identify his tribe from any tattoos, scars, or other indicators.

Rapidly, Gideon ran a list of Arizona Territory's first inhabitants, most of them decimated and removed to reservations now. He was aware of twenty, give or take, from Chemehuevi to Zuni—too many for him to play guessing games without more information to assist him.

And the simplest way to settle that, he knew, was just to ask.

"Waiting for me?"

The old man's voice, when he responded, was like parchment rubbed between a callused thumb and finger.

"You are special, Mr. Thorn."

"Thanks for the compliment. I don't recall us being introduced."

"Word of your coming travels on the wind."

"To anybody in particular?"

"I am Hania. It means Spirit Warrior in my people's tongue."

"Your people being, who?" asked Gideon.

"The Yaqui nation."

They were more common in Mexico, Thorn knew, throughout Sonora, but with scattered remnants spread across the territories of New Mexico and Arizona.

"Spirit Warrior is a shaman's name," Thorn said,

remembering that much from Harvard and his studies in the field of anthropology.

"No longer," Hania replied. "My time is past, or nearly so, but I still seek to help my people where I can."

Slowly approaching, fingers draped over the curved butt of his right-hand Peacemaker, Thorn took his room key from a vest pocket and held it in his left.

"You want to step inside?" he asked. "Or should we talk out here?"

"Inside, I think," the old man said. "These walls..."

"Have ears?" Gideon risked a smile. "My people have that saying, too."

Thorn kept an eye on Hania, his knife hand, while he plied the key and pushed the door open, glancing inside the room beyond to check for any more surprises there, then told his unexpected guest, "You first."

Inside the room, Gideon latched the door, a hedge against surprise intruders while he talked to the old Yaqui. There'd been no one else on station in the hallway but he could not say with certainty that other prowlers had not slipped into one of the rooms.

"You're not a lodger at the Continental," he began, remembering the Jim Crow sign downstairs, stating the obvious.

"No," Hania said. "And I have brought no others with me."

"Fair enough," Gideon said and nodded to the room's lone chair. "You want to have a seat?"

"Our business will not take that long."

"Do we have business?"

"You seek that which is responsible for killing settlers and their animals."

"Who told you that?" Gideon asked.

"I trust my eyes," Hania said. "You have *el nimbo,* as the Mexicans would say."

"Which is?"

"A glow, in terms that you might understand."

"First time I've heard that one," Gideon said.

"Only trained eyes can see it. You are marked as one who has seen much whether you always understand or not."

"I've seen some things," Gideon granted.

"Creatures of the flesh and of the mind."

"Where is this going?" Thorn inquired.

"Are you familiar with the *diablero*?" asked Hania.

"It's supposed to be some kind of Native spirit," Thorn replied. "Maybe a demon?"

"Or a golem as your Jews might say."

"They're not my Jews but I'm familiar with the golem, yes."

A legendary creature molded out of clay and brought to life, that was, in Hebrew legends, when removal of a threat was urgently required. Selected rabbis, it was said, had the power to mold a body out of clay, imbuing it with life until a mission was completed, then dismissing it back to the spiritual void from whence it came.

But Thorn had never met one in real life.

At least, not yet.

"Go on," he said. "I'm listening."

"Some of my people hate the settlers who have taken their ancestral lands."

"Some Yaquis. Would you count yourself among them?"

"Change will come, regardless of my feeling."

"So, you're thinking of some other shaman?"

"There is another," said his visitor.

"And you decided that I should be warned about him."

"If you stand in opposition to him," Hania replied. "But if I am mistaken..."

"Let's not jump the gun on that," Thorn cautioned. "What's this other shaman's name? Where might I find him?"

"Some questions I cannot answer," said Hania.

"But you came here to warn me," Gideon replied. "Saying, 'Some guy somewhere might do something' doesn't give me much to work on."

"First, I need to know you understand the risk and how to deal with it."

"So, fill me in."

"I tell you this," Hania answered. "Soon, perhaps tonight, the *diablero* will be conjured once again. Set free to work its master's will."

"Sounds like you're not too clear on where or when," Thorn noted.

"I cannot not see through another shaman's eyes," Hania said. "Once he has acted to invoke the spirits, I can sometimes feel him at his work. His malice marks him."

"Then you're certain it's a man, at least?"

"The Yaqui have no female shamans."

"Okay. How does that narrow down the field of suspects?"

"There are only two or three that I know of in Arizona Territory."

"Any others than yourself around Hades these days?"

"To speak a name when I cannot confirm it would be worse than slander in a white man's court of law."

"Worse than a string of murders?" Thorn pressed him.

The old Yaqui nodded silently.

"Well, if you know about me, then you understand this likely won't wind up in any court."

"I must be certain first," Hania said.

"All right," said Thorn. "In that case, bringing it to me was probably a waste of time for both of us."

"I had to warn someone."

"And you can't trust the law. I follow that," said Gideon. "But what you've shared with me won't get us anywhere."

"To face a *diablero* you must be prepared," Hania said.

"So, can you tell me that that might involve, at least?"

"To understand the shaman who has summoned it and his dark magic."

Thorn could only frown at that. "Forgive my saying so but you're talking in circles now."

"The world moves in a circle," said Hania. "And so does the spirit world."

"Uh-huh. How do I get in touch with you again if something happens?"

"I shall find you."

Gideon could only shrug at that. "I guess this is goodbye for now, then."

Opening his door, he watched Hania leave and move along the hotel corridor. Thorn felt an urge to trail him but he sensed the Yaqui would detect him and it might destroy his fragile sense of trust.

But trust in *what*?

His vague remarks brought Gideon no closer to the solution of the crimes he was investigating and, for all Thorn knew, Hania might never return to speak with him at all. In which case, he would be no better off than when he first arrived in Hades.

Gideon thought about a walk, maybe a stroll down to O'Grady's for some supper, but he had no appetite. Hania's convoluted warning, worse than useless to him, occupied Thorn's mind as he undressed for bed. He was no better off for having met the shaman—if Hania even *was* a shaman—than before they'd spoken. If the truth be told, his situation might even be worse.

As Thorn lay down, his twin Colts close beside him, his mind swirled with questions still unanswered. First and foremost, had Hania lied to him, misleading him deliberately? And if so, *why* make the effort? Thorn did not believe his visitor to be involved in conjuring a demon from beyond the earthly plane. Such things were possible, he knew from personal experience, but it would take a madman to reveal himself by indirection, thus inviting further scrutiny.

As for Hania spotting Thorn's "glow"—or *el nimbo*—Gideon supposed such things were possible, for someone with the powers of a psychic medium. Or, on the other hand, the Yaqui might have picked up rumors of a strange white man arriving in Hades. Hania didn't seem the type to read newspapers, certainly not papers published out of state that carried tales of Gideon's adventures chasing the unknown. But word of his arrival and his mission *could* have reached the old man's ears by other means.

And drawn him to do what, exactly?

That was where Thorn ran into a blank stone wall.

Perhaps he could discover a solution in his dreams.

Thinking of Dinah Pilcher far away, a sweet distraction from the mystery surrounding Hades, Thorn waited for sleep to find him, one hand resting lightly on the curved butt of his nearest Colt.

EIGHT

SOUTH OF HADES, PIMA COUNTY

Cha-time, a Yaqui shaman, knelt before the crackling campfire with his best friend and disciple Chu'a at his left hand. Reaching out with his right hand, Cha-time sprinkled something that resembled salt onto the fire, watching in satisfaction as the flames changed color from a reddish-orange to blue, shot through with streaks of ocher, green, and navy blue.

So far, so good.

Cha-time next began to chant a prayer of raising, each line echoed in its turn by a response Chu'a's lips. The summoning would take approximately fifteen minutes if it were successful. Failing that, Cha-time would be forced to try again.

His name, in English, was translated as "The Caller," chosen by his parents at Cha-time's birth, some thirty-seven summers earlier, after the shaman of their village marked the infant as a future shaman blessed with an ability to contact spirits on the Other Side, while working magic either light or dark.

Tonight's would be dark magic once again.

His comrade's name meant "Snake" in English, translated as *la culebra* or *la serpiente* into Spanish. What his parents had in mind was anybody's guess but the name suited Chu'a with his skill at secrecy and subterfuge.

Together, Cha-time believed that they could change the world—or, at the very least, their portion of it.

But the transformation would require more time.

They had been working on the recipe for two months now, progressing one step at a time, sowing the seeds of fear among homesteaders on the land Cha-time claimed as rightfully belonging to his people from time immemorial. With faith and time, he hoped the interlopers might be driven out entirely, or eradicated if they chose to stay and wage a losing battle against Fate.

The first invader, back in 1539, had been a solitary Spanish priest, Marcos de Niza. Rather than disposing of him instantly, the natives of what now was known as Arizona Territory let him roam at large, much like a plague germ floating on the desert breeze, followed by soldiers from his distant homeland seeking gold, erecting missions to convert the aboriginals to Christianity, excising or enslaving those who would not kneel to foreign gods beyond their comprehension. Over time, the Spaniards were expelled by mixed-breed *Mexicanos,* designated as a Mexican Empire, but soon transformed into a Federal Republic under presidents who aimed to pacify or massacre the red men standing in their way. Next came invaders from an upstart nation to the north, dubbed the United States, which stole nine hundred thousand square miles of

Northern Mexico at gunpoint, later paying the equivalent of seventeen dollars per square mile as a sop to the losers.

Nothing had changed for Cha-time's people or any other Native tribes during that span of centuries. Rather, it should be said that matters always went from bad to worse. Infection with disease, whether deliberate or accidental, paved the way for genocide by troops in varied uniforms and contract murders by scalp-hunters seeking bounties offered by Mexico City. Such bounties had a precedent in far-away New England, dating from the 18th century and carried on into the 1860s, during *El Norte*'s Civil War. By then, the Native warriors who had managed to survive, seeing their wives raped and their children carted off to boarding schools that stripped them of their born identities, were crowded onto "reservations" where their ranks were further thinned by plagues and alcohol—furnished by white bootleggers acting in conjunction with the politicians who had ruled its sale to "Indians" illegal.

Across those generations, certain war chiefs had rebelled against the foreign onslaught. In the Southwest, those included Cochise and Alcala, Black Knife and Geronimo, "Big Foot" Massai and Mangas Coloradas. Each in turn, and others like them, had been run to ground and murdered or coerced into surrendering and living out their final days on barren land no white man cared to claim.

But times were changing now, thanks to Cha-time and Chu'a. At long last, after all the many generations of their people beaten down and disinherited, robbed of their land, their children and their culture, even their ancestral gods and rituals, within a country that was founded on the promise of "religious freedom," the invaders from Europe, together with their subject classes brought from Africa and

Asia to be slaves in fields and mines, would see a new world rising in their midst.

Or, rather, they would face an *old* world born again, asserting dominance as it was always meant to be.

Cha-time's modest moves so far in Arizona Territory were the first steps toward that revolutionary change. Other shamans from other tribes would sense his power, given time, and would undoubtedly pursue their own paths to recovery.

For now, it was enough to wage a local war and see the red man's enemies recoil in horror.

Rising from the multi-colored flames before Chat-time and Chu'a, the air began to shimmer now. Their chanting grew in volume as the *diablero*'s form took shape, changing from mist into a solid form with strength enough to rend and kill its chosen prey.

And there was no shortage of targets to be harvested.

HADES

Marshal Brett Ruggles paused outside of Diamond Lil's saloon and peered in through its broad front window from the darkened thoroughfare of Easy Street. He watched the gamblers at their card tables, drinkers lining the bar, and painted ladies circulating in their nightly search for randy customers to follow them upstairs.

No trouble there, so far, although he might be called upon before midnight to roust a rowdy drunk or two.

These days—and more particularly nights—it seemed townsfolk were drinking more than usual, to drown their fears of whatever was lurking just beyond the posted limits of their settlement, haunting the dark desert waste.

And, as the marshal knew full well from listening to whispers around town, masking the fear that whatever "it" was, the creeping terror might run out of victims in the countryside and start to prowl their town.

If that happened, Ruggles would be confronted with a Hobson's choice of fleeing for his life or standing fast against a nightmare he had yet to fully comprehend. Take it or leave it, as the saying went. Desert the people he had sworn to serve and to protect or make himself a human sacrifice.

Of one thing he was certain: there would be no help forthcoming from the Pima County sheriff's office based in Tucson. Charley Shibell had always been a politician first and lawman second, thinking first of his career and its advancement, solving cases that were easy or which threatened his prospects for reelection before tackling mysteries that made him break a sweat. He might dispatch a deputy or two if things got any worse, to have a look around and file reports that blamed the crimes on drifting border trash or Mexicans.

In Arizona Territory, race would always be a prime consideration in assigning guilt, even if that meant manufacturing sufficient "evidence" to dupe an all-white jury while it sent a blameless brown or red man to the gallows.

Moving on from Diamond Lil's to have a look-in at The Prairie Dog, Ruggles wondered what sort of help he might expect from the stranger called Gideon Thorn. The marshal had discussed their visitor with Ellis Flynn, who'd followed Thorn's career in print and was considering a front-page story on him for the *Hades Flame.* Ruggles had discouraged that, at least for now, reminding Flynn that any more discussion of the supernatural would only agitate townspeople further and make life more difficult.

As if it weren't already bad enough.

Outside the town's second saloon, the marshal paused again, scanning the patrons gathered under reassuring lamplight while the rest of Hades lay in darkness. Shops and offices were closed at dusk these days, lights showing only from behind drawn curtains in the quarters of proprietors who lived upstairs. Homes like the clapboard house that Ruggles rented mostly stood in darkness too, their occupants gone off to bed early, keeping their guns nearby, to toss and turn in grim anticipation of another day ahead.

Commerce was down and that was pinching everyone as Ruggles knew from the complaints he had received of late. It was beyond his understanding, what shopkeepers thought a marshal could accomplish to relieve their economic suffering. It was beyond his power, obviously, to drag patrons off the street and force them to make purchases they neither needed nor desired.

The only items selling well of late, aside from booze and sex at the saloons, were guns and ammunition flying off the shelves at Harry Delray's hardware store. When those ran out, trade ran toward hunting knives and axes, anything a worried man, woman, or child might hope to wield in self-defense.

The mayhem had not laid a bloody hand on Hades yet, but it was turning into an armed camp prepared for battle. Against what? No one aside from Pastor Blake held any strong opinion on that subject yet, and he was blaming Satan, counting on that bogeyman to fill Sunday collection plates.

So far, Ruggles had no idea precisely who or what to blame for the calamity infesting his corner of Pima County but he seriously doubted his ability to stem the plague without a skillful helping hand. Whether the black-clad stranger with an interest in all things supernatural would be the owner of that hand, the marshal could not say. One thing was certain, though.

He'd had no other offers yet, so Thorn would have to do unless a better option happened to present itself, and soon.

Moving along on past The Prairie Dog saloon, Ruggles tried doorknobs of the shops and offices he passed, ensuring that each one was duly locked against the night. Ahead and on his right, the dark mouth of an alley yawned between Joe Chatsworth's dry goods store and Amos Grundy's barbershop. Avoiding it, the marshal stepped down from the wooden sidewalk he's been following and gave himself some space, moving with measured strides down the middle of Easy Street.

"Damned scaredy cat," he muttered to himself, then masked it with a smile.

Unconsciously, he glanced up toward the Continental Hotel's second story, where he knew Gideon Thorn was lodged. No lamp was burning in the hunter's room and since Ruggles had seen no trace of him in either of the town's saloons—and banking on the fact that Gideon would not be laid up with some harlot, paying by the hour —Ruggles guessed that he'd turned in already.

Passing the hostelry on his way home, Ruggles wished Thorn a peaceful night and pleasant dreams, if such a thing were even possible in Pima County nowadays.

EAST OF HADES, PIMA COUNTY

Hania sat silently before the embers of a dying fire and stared beyond them into darkness that seemed limitless, a void spanning the territory, possibly the world itself. Behind his eyes and in the pumping muscles of his heart, the shaman felt a stirring he'd been waiting for since sundown, trolling for it with his open mind.

Evil was on the move, made manifest in something close to human form, but larger and more powerful.

A demon was abroad tonight. If only he could work out where it came from and the destination it was seeking.

More important still, Hania yearned to know who had the twisted power and the malice in his soul required to call it forth.

How else could he hope to assist that man called Thorn in frustrating an unnamed plotter's scheme?

The candidates Hania had in mind were three in number. One, the eldest shaman, was named Ahtahkakoop —"star blanket" in English—and Hania had discounted him as harmless, being close to death at eighty-seven winters old and known to be a pacifist. The second, Dahkeya—"eternal," as his parents named him—was approaching sixty-five years old and had renounced opposing whites by violence after war chief Flechas Rayadas died fighting the U.S. Cavalry outside Pilar, New Mexico, in April 1854. That left Cha-time as the list's most likely candidate but Hania would not accuse a fellow shaman without solid proof in hand.

He owed a fellow worshiper that much, at least.

And there might still be someone else whom he had overlooked, perhaps a new arrival in the territory bent on literally raising Hell.

At any given time, there were at least a few score Yaqui warriors, mostly young and relatively inexperienced at battling with intruders, who might fall in line behind a self-styled revolutionary shaman and make things worse for their people in the process. Hania felt no less anger toward the settlers who had robbed his fellow Yaquis of their hopes and land than any other self-respecting tribesmen, but he'd come to terms with what was possible, versus a futile shouting at the gods for vengeance when the time for that had passed.

A tremor rippled through Hania's body, as he knelt before the bed of glowing coals, as if an ice-cold hand had clutched his nape and sent a shiver racing down his spine. He recognized that feeling, understood its meaning, and controlled his heaving stomach with an effort.

Somewhere, not too many miles away, the ritual for summoning a *diablero* was complete. Whoever called it from the Dark Beyond, the demon had achieved physical form and was receiving its instructions from its shaman master.

That, Hania knew, was bad on two levels. First and most obvious, the creature would be tasked to hunt and slay another human target, leaving bloody mayhem in its wake. Worse yet, if Hania's suspicions were correct, each time its earthly master called it forth, the *diablero* gained more power, striving toward the point where it could operate without relying on the shaman who believed—mistakenly—that he could dabble in dark magic and control it without any consequences for himself.

When that time came, the menace would be infinitely worse. A monster with a boundless thirst for blood would be unleashed, acting without direction from a guiding hand. There was no telling who it might attack, even the

Yaquis it was first called up to serve without their knowledge. Once the *diablero* turned upon its earthly master and destroyed him, it could run amok at random, mingling evil with insanity beyond the scope of any healer's power to restrain it.

In that case, Hania feared that there would be no stopping it short of a grim apocalyptic ending which no seer could predict.

Slumping before the remnants of his fire, Hania wavered on the hazy border between dreams and madness. He could feel the *diablero* stalking its intended prey but could not name the next intended victims or direct help to them in whatever time they still had left. Before he could mount up and travel back to Hades, find Gideon Thorn and tell him what was happening, it would already be too late for those in peril.

And, in any case, Hania could not point Thorn to the site where blood would soon be spilled.

Feeling disgusted with himself, Hania pulled a blanket up around his shoulders, lay down near the fire pit, waiting for unconsciousness to carry him away.

Perhaps in dreams, if nowhere else, his questions might be answered even if he failed to halt another tragedy.

HADES

At that same moment, Thorn was also dreaming in his bedroom on the second story of the Continental Hotel overlooking Easy Street. More precisely, he was trapped inside a nightmare, longing to escape but with no power to break free.

Thorn's dream had started off nicely enough with images of Dinah Pilcher traveling beside him, jotting down the details of his travels for posterity. They'd met for the first time in California's San Diego County, where Dinah was publisher and editor of a small newspaper, the *Sagrado Sentinel.* Thorn was immersed, as usual, in trying to resolve a murder mystery that led him into conflict with a tiny remnant of the ancient Aztec empire bent on summoning dark forces to eradicate its earthly enemies.

The echoes of that case reverberated through Hania's warning of a Yaqui shaman bent on similar results and virtually ensured that Thorn would pass a restless night, pursued by demons through his dreams.

As usual, of course, whenever he lay down to sleep and dreamt of Dinah Pilcher, it began quite pleasantly. During their time together, mutual respect had blossomed into cautious intimacy, each of them strongly attracted to the other, neither willing to forsake the callings which had brought them into contact. Dinah had come close to death during their first adventure but she'd worked through that, assisting Gideon's attempt to solve an early childhood memory of brutal loss, then took off on her own to probe a case of grave-robbing that jeopardized her life and sanity before Thorn intervened to save her from a ghastly living death.

Since then, she'd been recovering in Boston and her latest letter indicated that she hoped to reunite with Gideon in the near future. That should have been good news but it also resurrected apprehension on Thorn's part that any further contact might be the last straw for Dinah, pushing her beyond the limits of what any human mind and body could endure.

Thorn's nightmare, thus, turned out to be a grim, surrealistic melding of his early days in Dinah's company and the bizarre events which had been terrorizing Pima County. From pleasant memories of grappling with her on a rumpled bed, his mind segued to facing remnants of the ancient Aztec culture based on human sacrifice, slaying a monster from the dawn of time that had annihilated Thorn's loved ones when he was barely two years old, and, finally, a showdown with a pack of zombies in the hinterlands of Arkansas.

When he woke, sitting bolt upright in his rented bed and sheathed with perspiration, Thorn discovered that he clutched a Colt in either hand, their hammers cocked. Another moment, lost within the panic of his dreams, and he might have discharged those pistols, peppering the Continental's walls, perhaps wounding or killing strangers in adjacent rooms. Taking a moment to relax and breathe deeply, he eased those hammers down, first one Colt, then the other, and returned them to their holsters, setting them atop a nightstand to his right.

Next, Thorn rolled out of bed and washed his face, using a basin and pitcher of water that the hotel had provided. Drying with a fluffy towel, he stripped the damp sheets from his bed and let them drop onto the carpet, they lay back again and plumped his pillow, waiting for his mind and body to relax.

Outside, on Easy Street, he heard a group of men squabbling and laughing as they exited The Prairie Dog saloon. Thorn briefly thought of Marshal Ruggles, wondered whether he was sleeping well tonight, then felt his mind stray back to Dina Pilcher in Boston and tried to shut that down before it got ahold of him again.

Still dark outside and hours more to go before sunrise. If there was devilry afoot in Pina County Thorn had likely missed it, lost in dark realms of his own. If an atrocity were waiting for him in the morning, he would think about it then. He hated that it might require another massacre to put him on the scent of whoever or *what*ever he'd come to find but that was a familiar feeling in his quest to sort out the unknown.

Thorn might be able to communicate with certain animals by means most men would never recognize but he could not divine the secrets kept within a human mind or heart. Hania might return with further information in his own good time but, meanwhile, Thorn was on his own, unable to impart the Yaqui shaman's hints to Marshal Ruggles without seeming like a fool.

Whether they cracked the mystery in time to head off further innocent bloodshed, Gideon guessed that Hades had not seen its last death yet before the issue was resolved. And if he died while chasing the solution, then what?

Giving up on sleep for now, Thorn rose and lit the room's sole lamp, removed a writing pad and pencil from his saddlebags, and sat down at a small desk overlooking East Street. Over the next half hour, he prepared a note to Dinah Pilcher, planning not to mail it until Pima County's mystery was solved.

And failing that, Ruggles could always post it for him.

That is, if the lawman managed to survive.

NINE

WEST OF HADES

Ernie Fletcher had not a peaceful moment with his family since he'd discovered Jack and Sonya Conyers mutilated on their ranch and carried that grim news to Marshal Ruggles in Hades. He dared not sleep, fearing what might be creeping up on him, his wife Clarice, and their two sons, Matthew and Vincent.

During daylight hours, meanwhile, Ernie still had all his chores around the ranch to finish which had driven him to near-exhaustion. If the tension did not let up soon, he would be hard pressed to avoid total collapse.

But if he left his guard down even for a second, Ernie knew the consequences might be infinitely worse.

Clarice, bless her heart, had tried to talk him out of fretting constantly, reminding him that so far, no two raids had struck adjacent spreads, but what did that prove? No one knew whether the slaughter had been caused by animals or people so it did no good trying to read the perpetrators' minds.

And Ernie had already seen their handiwork with his own eyes.

No matter if he lived to be a hundred, there was no forgetting that.

So Ernie Fletcher worked by day and watched over his family at night. He never left their house without at least one firearm on his person and, at night, he carried two. His sidearm was an old LeMat revolver used by the Confederacy in the Civil War. It weighed four pounds and measured just a smidgen over thirteen inches, holding nine .42-caliber rounds in its cylinder. The kicker was a second barrel for a twenty-gauge shotgun shell, which had earned the gun its nickname as the "grape shot revolver" and a lethal killer at close range.

For night patrols, Ernie added a Henry lever-action rifle, chambered for .44-caliber rimfire rounds, packing fifteen cartridges inside its magazine plus one more in the chamber. That made twenty-six rounds before Ernie had to reload either of his guns and if he couldn't stop an enemy with all that firepower, then...

Which was the problem as he saw it.

Jack Conyers, the night he died, was similarly armed, with a Winchester "Yellow Boy," backed by a Smith & Wesson six-gun. Ernie knew his neighbor as a crack shot yet he had been butchered—torn apart, no less—by some unknown intruder on his property that managed to escape intact. Likewise, Jack's widow had been carrying a Colt revolver when the same attacker ripped her limb from limb and she had not been able to defend herself successfully. Indeed, there was no sign that either Jack or Sonya had any injury upon their killer, though with so much blood spattered across their farmyard, who could say?

By moonlight, Fletcher checked his pocket watch, an

heirloom passed down from his grandfather before Eddie had left Kentucky looking for a fresh start in the Arizona Territory. Things had been unsettled in those days after the Civil Way, particularly in a former slave state that had never broken with the Union. For ten years, he had made a halfway decent living from the arid land until the present plague had settled over Pima County like a brooding bank of storm clouds that might never lift for all he knew.

It was too late to leave and try another new start somewhere farther west, much less return with drooping tail between his legs to pick up where he'd left off in the Blue Grass State. Circling the farmyard now, exhausted, Eddie Fletcher knew that he must make his last stand here and either win through to preserve his family and humble home or die in the attempt.

Clarice Fletcher loved her sons beyond measure but there was no denying that the little tykes were grating on her nerves these past few days. Matthew was nine years old, his brother Vincent six, just learning how to help around the house and ranch before their father spotted trouble at the Conyers place and everything they'd worked for over time began to fall apart.

That wasn't strictly fair, she realized, no more than blaming Eddie for the fact that he had stumbled on to Jack and Sonya on the morning after they were butchered, but *fair* didn't always enter into private feelings. As she moved around the kitchen, shooing Matt and Vince out of her way impatiently, Clarice wished that her husband had not noticed anything while he was riding past the Conyers' spread, had missed it altogether and let someone else carry the tale on into town.

Not that it would have spared them from the grim anxiety Clarice had lived with every moment since that time.

The trouble hadn't started out with Jack and Sonya, friends of hers and Eddie's, nor was their slaughter the end of it. Proximity to the disaster naturally made Clarice worry that she and hers might be the next in line although there'd been no pattern to the killings so far, happening around Hades at what seemed like a list of randomly selected sites.

That didn't help, of course, and Eddie hadn't managed more than two, three hours sleep per night in the meantime. He labored all day long around the ranch, feeding and watering the stock, making repairs to fill whatever time their animals did not demand, and then spent most of each night on patrol with guns to keep the lurking menace from their doorstep.

For her part, Clarice cleaned up around the house as usually, prepared three meals a day, and kept her Model 1861 Colt Navy pistol close at hand, loaded with .38-caliber rimfire rounds that should stop any man in his tracks.

Clarice's fear, of course, was that the prowling killer might not be a man at all.

There had been talk of savage animals involved although the species had not been identified and, from what Eddie shared with her about the Conyers murder scene, it didn't sound like any beast Clarice had ever heard of prowling Pima County. They had black bears and coyotes, the odd mountain lion now and then, but all of them were generally shy of humankind and could be slain with guns in able hands. For any one of them to kill four people and so many livestock without anybody spotting it or getting off a kill shot strained all credibility.

She had to wonder now if there was something to the rumors coming out of Hades, mostly from the Mercy Baptist Church, blaming some kind of evil spirit for the killings, maybe even Satan his own self.

Clarice had never put much stock in church per se and she shared Eddie's view that any cash they managed to accumulate would serve them better than some pastor with his hand out but the unrelenting onslaught scouring southern Pima County had begun to give her second thoughts.

Why here? Why now?

What had her neighbors done to bring Hell down upon their heads?

"Matthew, stop bothering your brother!" she demanded, sending Matt into a pout. The strain, she knew, was more than any child could stand but that was true of everyone. Until the mystery was solved, stress would remain a constant in their isolated lives and all of them would simply have to live with it.

A haunting thought intruded on her mind then, Clarice frowning as she heard a small voice whispering inside her head, *Assuming that we live at all.*

Cha-time followed the *diablero*'s progress with his mind, imagining the view from its eyes as it strode across the open desert toward its target. That perspective was disorienting since the demon stood two feet or more taller than Cha-time so that the shaman felt as if he were walking on stilts.

A buzzing in Cha-time's ears distracted him as if a pesky gnat were circling around his head. Unconsciously, he grimaced, realizing that it must be Chu'a's voice distracting him when he could least afford the interruption.

Making no attempt to hide his irritation in that moment, Cha-time half turned toward Chu'a, snapping at him. "What?"

"I asked how your attempt at mastering control is coming?"

"It would be easier without your yammering," Cha-time answered back.

"Forgive me, Caller," Chu'a muttered not quite sullenly.

Cha-time cared nothing about Snake's mood just now. Only his silence was required.

In truth, the first few times that Cha-time had called the *diablero* forth, he had communicated his desire—eradication of all interlopers from the Arizona Territory—but had been unable to direct its movements more specifically. The demon needed blood to motivate it after crossing over from the Other Side, originally satisfied with that of sheep and cattle, then progressing to the stronger vital force of men. Only the last time had Cha-time managed to direct it more or less and that required its summoning within the line of sight for an intended target.

But tonight felt better to Cha-time. He had settled on the rancher who'd discovered his most recent victims, knowing that the busybody's death and slaughter of his nearest kin would amplify anxiety among the other homesteaders he wished to terrorize and banish from Yaqui ancestral lands. In time, Cha-time reckoned he could send the *diablero* into Hades, moving through its streets and leaving only death behind.

But that still lay ahead of him. Cha-time's war to

cleanse the desert of intruders would take time. It might cost him his life, in fact, but sacrifice was often necessary to achieve a worthwhile goal. How many of his fellow tribesmen had been murdered while resisting the invasion of their sacred hunting grounds?

Cha-time meant to raise that number on the other side, prepare his *diablero* to fight on without him if Cha-time fell along the way and see the campaign through to final victory.

If he was granted time, he might even direct the spirit warrior north to Tucson, where the white lords clung to Pima County's reins, directing politics and commerce as decreed from Phoenix and beyond it, all the way to Washington, D.C.

It was too much to hope, perhaps, that he could purge the continent of foul invaders from across the sea but Cha-time's honor compelled him to attempt great things. The more opponents he dispatched with his dark magic, the more his reputation would be amplified among his ancestors when he passed on to join them in the Happy Hunting Grounds.

Whenever that transpired, Cha-time meant to be prepared but, first, he had more work to do on Earth, bleeding his enemies until the desert soil ran red.

Eddie Fletcher felt his stomach tighten as he heard a growling sound behind his barn. It could be anything, of course—the desert night was rife with predators and scavengers—but, from experience, he judged it must be something larger than the average coyote and he knew that gray wolf populations had been dwindling steadily with the advance of sheep and cattle ranching in the territory. As for cougars, it had been three years since Fletcher had heard reports of any in the area and five years since he'd glimpsed one briefly on his property.

What, then? The only thing that came to Eddie's mind was *trouble* that he could not name with any certainty. Something whose work he'd seen before, and recently.

Advancing on the barn with cautious strides, he eased the Henry rifle's hammer back as quietly as he could manage, grimacing at the inevitable *click* that told him it was cocked. He kept his index finger well outside the trigger guard but close enough that he could fire within a fraction of a second as required.

And once he started shooting, Fletcher would not stop until he stood over the carcass of a kill, whatever it might prove to be.

Assuming that a gun could do the job.

He thought again about the hardware Jack and Sonya Conyers had been carrying the night they died and clenched his teeth against a sudden chill entirely unrelated to the desert night. Eddie fought a sudden urge to run back for the house and lock himself inside, wait out the night and never mind what happened to his stock, but that was not a man's way of resolving anything in Arizona Territory. Here, a fellow stood his ground and either fought it out or died trying and left a memory his missus could be proud of once she'd planted him.

It was an unforgiving land for hard, uncompromising men.

Another snarl reached Fletcher's ears and he proceeded, turned his mind off to the shameful trembling in his hands, and went to find out what in holy Hell was going on.

Hania could not make a personal connection with the *diablero*—no one but the shaman who had summoned it possessed that power—but his instinct told him that it was about to strike and not too many miles from where he knelt in darkness, chanting softly to his ancestors across the void.

Another homestead was in jeopardy and, while Hania could not ward it off, there was a chance that if he reached the scene in time—before the magic faded into desert daylight—he might still learn something more about the demon's origin and who controlled it on the earthly plane.

And once he knew that absolutely, could he send Gideon Thorn to stop it?

Could a white man even hope to end its reign of terror?

Chanting to the moon and stars, Hania wondered if his ancestors could even hear him or if they would listen sympathetically to his entreaties. It was possible, the agent Yaqui thought, that he was out of step with the intention of his forefathers. If they desired the *diablero* and empowered it, then he was helpless to prevent its running wild through Prima County and beyond.

And come to that, why should he care if interloping settlers were eradicated from the territory. What did he owe to ranchers, whether they were white, black, or Hispanic? All of them, in Hania's experience, despised him and the remnant of his people. It could only benefit the Yaquis if their lifelong enemies were swept away.

But after that was done, what happened next?

What would prevent the shaman who had called it forth from sending it against his own tribe, weeding out whichever Yaquis would not bow and worship him in turn?

No.

Hania could not permit that sacrilege. He must oppose it and, if possible, expunge it from the land. If that required a skillful white man's aid, so be it.

And if that cost Hania his life, what still remained of it, then it was worth the risk.

Eddie Fletcher circled around his barn with quiet, cautious strides. He kept his Henry rifle shouldered now, ready to fire immediately if a shadow crossed his path, wishing that he could have another moment with Clarice and their two boys, warning them all to stay inside the house and not come out until daybreak no matter what they heard.

No matter how he screamed.

His circuit of the barn revealed nothing until Fletcher had reached its rear, facing northeast. Unlike the front, where double doors permitted him to liberate his stock at dawn and bed them down at nightfall, Eddie's other entrance to the building was man-sized, secured with a latch on the inside that opened when he pulled a hank of rope protruding from a hole around eye level. Tugging that allowed the access door to open inward on its well-oiled hinges, silently, while Fletcher slipped inside.

Tonight, he let his Henry's muzzle lead the way, prepared for anything that might transpire. In truth, he had no clue what to expect, particularly since both entries to the barn were properly secured—the double doors out front barred by a sturdy beam on the outside, the smaller one still latched as he had left it when the sun went down.

Of course, he realized, a prowler could have freed that lock from the outside, as he was doing now, then shut and latched the door again on the inside, but he had seen the

Conyers farmyard carnage for himself and doubted that a human mind—a sane one, anyway—had carried out that massacre. Standing in darkness at the backdoor's threshold, Eddie could not imagine that bloodthirsty predator plotting subtle strategic moves.

And yet, the last snarl he had heard seemed to emerge from somewhere *inside* Fletcher's barn.

When no one tried to snatch the Henry from his hands, Eddie reached up with his left hand to find the lantern he kept hanging on a peg there, around shoulder level. His next move, lighting that lamp, would briefly leave him vulnerable since he had to prop his rifle up against the door jamb, pull a box of matches from his overalls, and kindle some illumination for his search inside the barn.

No problem, Eddie silently advised himself, with the LeMat revolver holstered on his belt. If anyone or any*thing* appeared to move while he was at it, he could draw and blast the prowler ten times at close range, then snatch his rifle and repeat the exercise.

In fact, he lit the lantern without incident and heard his animals shifting uneasily inside their stalls, the cattle lowing, sheep bleating. He spoke aloud to them, using the soft voice they preferred, and raised the lamp, immediately brightening the barn's gloomy interior.

When nothing rushed to meet him, Fletcher started to relax a bit, though not entirely. Taking up his rifle once again, its buttstock wedged between his right elbow and ribs, he backed up far enough to shut the barn's backdoor and heard its latch drop into place. Before him, nothing moved except the livestock, making Eddie wonder if the growls inside the barn were simply his imagination running wild.

Better a slight case of hysterics than a battle for his life.

At fifteen feet inside the barn, its hayloft overshadowed Fletcher. Having scanned the ground floor left to right and back again, he turned to face the loft, his Henry's muzzle rising with his gaze to sweep the platform overhead—and that was when it happened.

Something large—no, make that *huge*—dropped down in front of him, disdaining contact with the wooden ladder to his right. At first, he thought it was a man, at least six-five, but as it landed with a wheezing grunt Fletcher knew that initial estimate of size was wrong.

Dead wrong.

The thing looming before him was no less than seven feet in height, perhaps taller than that, and while it stood revealed in lamplight, Fletcher recognized its manlike form —two legs, two arms, one head—but all out of proportion to his own respectable five-ten. The arms that reached for Eddie matched a fat man's thighs for girth. Its hands, the size of skillets, had fingers as thick as sausages, each tipped with black talons resembling a bear's.

Fletcher fired once into the monster's chest at point-blank range, smelled flesh scorching before one of those giant hands disarmed him, flung the Henry into shadow, while the other closed over his face. Groping to reach his pistol, Eddie felt tremendous pressure on his skull before it crumpled like an eggshell and his senses dissipated in a flash of swarming sparks.

He never felt the lamp fall from his dead left hand or smash between his boots, was gone before its flames leaped to his overalls and flickered upward to devour him.

"That's Daddy's gun!" Matt Fletcher yelped.

"Hush now," Clarice admonished him, turning toward Vincent as she added on, "The both of you!"

Hustling her sons aside, she bolted to the nearest window, peered out through its gun slit, and saw firelight flickering inside the barn through gaps between its weathered sideboards. When the rifle shot was not repeated, as the glow of flames burned brighter and their animals began to panic, Clarice turned upon her sons.

"Get in your bedroom now," she ordered. "Hide under the beds and don't come out until I call your names."

"Yes, ma'am," Matthew replied, dragging his younger brother after him and out of sight, shutting their bedroom door. Vincent was starting to protest when Matthew gave his arm a yank and silenced him, playing his role of elder brother to the hilt.

They were good boys at heart, though often mischievous. Grabbing her Navy Colt, Clarice wondered how she would raise them without Eddie's guiding hand. That thought was instantly supplanted by another—namely, whether any of them would survive the night at all.

Tears nearly blinded her as Clarice peered out through the window's gun slit once again but she would not succumb to fear. Not while there was a chance for Eddie to emerge alive and racing from the barn to join her. He was brave as any other five men she could name, all rolled together, but the lack of any further gunfire from the barn, coupled with smoke escaping from the hayloft now, made Clarice fear the worst.

Five minutes passed and she could hear the shrill screams of their animals trapped in the barn, when suddenly its two front doors burst open, swinging wide apart as if propelled by a stampede. Instead of fleeing cows and sheep, however, Clarice saw a giant manlike figure wreathed in flame and smoke emerge into the barnyard, size and form distorted by firelight, casting a giant shadow as it lumbered toward the house on legs as thick as tree trunks.

"Dear Jesus God!" she whispered. She cocked her Navy Colt and backed off from the window, from their front door, stopping in the kitchen only when her rump collided with the stove.

She was braced there, hissing at her sons for silence in their bedroom, when the front door burst open, framing the massive figure from their farmyard, still in flames that made its face obscure and wavering although apparently unburned. As it advanced across the sitting room to reach her, with its fiery footsteps leaving charred marks on the floorboards, Clarice raised her Colt and tucked its muzzle underneath her chin.

At that point, nothing mattered but to keep those groping, burning hands away from her.

TEN

HADES: SEPTEMBER 8, 1877

Thorn chose O'Grady's for breakfast on Saturday morning. The waitress still came out to greet him with a practiced smile but early diners in the restaurant seemed more suspicious of him, verging on hostile, than they had been over the past two days.

That came as no surprise since things were heating up in southern Pima County and the mayhem stalking homesteads in the neighborhood had echoes along Easy Street in Hades.

One early customer seated alone was Pastor Blake from Mercy Baptist, seated with his head down over sausage and fried eggs, his high-crowned parson's hat resting beside his plate and coffee cup. He made a point of concentrating on his food while Thorn passed by his table, moving toward a table set for two beside the solitary window facing toward the thoroughfare.

With his back turned to the hostile room, Thorn ordered creamed chipped beef on toast, potatoes on the side, with coffee, strong and black. After the night he'd passed, Gideon wanted something that would keep him wide awake until lunchtime when he might stop in for some spicy offering from Casa del Sol's grill.

Assuming that he was not interrupted in the meantime by another helping of bad news.

In fact, he'd nearly cleaned his plate when he glanced up and saw Brett Ruggles crossing East Street from the direction of the Continental, spotting Gideon and picking up his pace to dodge a buckboard rattling past. Gaining the sidewalk, Ruggles paused and tipped his hat in greeting to a pair of bustling housewives out for early morning rounds, then stepped into O'Grady's, nodding toward Thorn's table so the waitress would not follow him. Gideon's fellow diners tracked the lawman as he passed them, torn between staring and feigning ignorance of his arrival.

"You're out early," Ruggles said, settling into the empty chair across from Thorn.

"Up and at it for another day in Hades," Gideon replied.

Eyeing his plate, the marshal said, "Looks like you're just about ready to go."

"You have someplace we need to be?" asked Thorn, feeling the last bite of his breakfast settle heavily behind his belt buckle.

"Wish I could tell you, 'No'," Ruggles replied. "But yeah, there's been more trouble overnight."

"Another homestead?"

"Used to be. From what I understand, there's not much of it left."

"Meaning?"

"Sounds like they had a fire. The house and barn combined. Seems like nobody made it out."

"That's different," Thorn said.

"We won't know that until we have a look," said Ruggles.

"Someone you know, I guess."

"You knew him, too," the marshal answered. "Eddie Fletcher, plus his wife and boys."

"All four?"

"From what I hear." Ruggles glanced past Thorn, checking out the room. "Why don't we finish this outside?"

O'Grady's other diners dropped all pretense of indifference as Thorn rose, paid his bill, and left the waitress a substantial tip. Outside, on Easy Street, it felt to him as if each passerby were shooting sidelong glances his way or it may have been the marshal who provoked their curiosity.

In either case, Gideon knew the bad news had already worked its way through Hades or, if not, would soon complete the circuit, each retelling grown more terrible as it went on.

"Who tipped you off?" he asked Ruggles.

"Same thing as with the Conyers family. An early-rising neighbor passing by. This one was heading out of town but changed his mind and high-tailed into to see me once he saw the smoke. He was afraid to take a closer look and I can't say I blame him."

Eddie Fletcher had reported the last tragedy and, now, his brood had been the next targets. News like that would make the rounds and farmers in the area would be afraid of stepping far away from home with it in mind.

"He stayed clear of the scene, though?" Gideon inquired.

"That's what he said," Ruggles confirmed. "Saw just

enough to tell the house and barn were both in ashes. Likely packing up his wife and kids by this time, clearing out."

Gideon thought about his Yaqui visitor from yesterday, his tale of a rogue shaman using magic in a bid to drive away unwelcome homesteaders. He thought of telling Ruggles that but then decided he was better off keeping it to himself, at least for now. With tension running high already, Yaquis didn't need a gang of vigilantes shaping up to run them off—or worse.

"We're heading out there, then?" Thorn asked.

"Soon as we're saddled up. I've got the undertaker and his sidekick gearing up and Doc Maddox is standing by to have a look at the remains soon as Primm brings them in."

"Okay," Thorn said. "You want to meet me at the livery?"

"Be there in ten," Ruggles confirmed and strode off toward his office where his bay mare stood waiting, its reins tied to the hitching rail in front.

Thorn walked down to the livery and greeted Monte Rifkin at his morning chores.

"More trouble overnight, I hear," the hostler said.

"Sounds like it."

A glum nod in response. "I'll get your stallion ready."

Thorn communed with Belle and Shadow silently while helping Rifkin at his task of saddling the stallion. Shadow didn't mind a morning ride, while Belle, as usual, seemed happy just to stay indoors with feed and water readily available. Marshal Ruggles had arrived as Gideon walked Shadow from the stable onto East Street and mounted up.

They headed out of town together, in the same direction that they'd followed to the Conyers spread before, sharp eyes in every shop along the way watching them pass, minds focused on the latest horror Hades and its residents had to endure.

Hania found the Fletcher ranch before Ruggles and Thorn, trailed by the undertaker's wagon, reached the scene. For some reason, a murder site revealed itself more easily to him by daylight than in darkness, even though Hania felt it should have been the other way around when his demonic enemy was still at work.

This time, when he was still a mile or more distant, the Yaqui shaman could smell ashes on the morning breeze, and roasted flesh from more than one species of animal.

Closing the gap, Hania had no clue who owned the former ranch, laid to waste now, beyond understanding that they had been white and thus no friends of his. That said, he would not have desired for them to die in flames or torn apart by *diablero* fangs and talons, even in the cause of winning back his tribe's ancestral homeland.

Change was natural, if not always desirable, but meddling with dark forces from the supernatural was not the best way of affecting it in Hania's experience. Shamans sometimes forgot their place within the broader scheme of things, beyond tending to wounds and illness or interpreting visions and dreams. When one of them set out to change the course of history laid down by Fate, the end result was often worse than the conspiracies of rich men in their smoke-filled boardrooms far away.

And what was happening of late in Pima County went beyond unnatural into the realm of magic twisted to pursuit of personal reward.

In all his years to date, Hania had seen nothing good result from such an exercise.

And of the bad examples he could cite offhand, the present plague in Arizona Territory was by far the worst.

He reached the blighted, burned-out homestead as two riders were approaching, recognizing both of them on sight. One, riding a black stallion, was the man he'd spoken to last night at the hotel in town. The other, on a bay mare, was the town's lawman, although his name eluded Hania. Behind them, trailing at a range of thirty yards or so, he recognized an undertaker's wagon laden with pine boxes to receive the charred remnants of three—no, four—white settlers who had been incinerated overnight. Hania could no longer sense their pain, which thankfully had dissipated, but he had a fair idea of what they'd suffered from the scene laid out before him.

Cautiously, he laid down in the dry brown grass to watch and wait.

"See what I mean?" Brett Ruggles asked as they approached the Fletcher spread.

"Nobody lived through that," Thorn granted, sounding weary more than anything.

The former barn and house had been reduced to mounds of smoking ash, stray beams protruding here and there like black accusatory fingers pointing rudely toward the desert sky.

Ruggles turned and called back to the wagon following behind them. "Better let us check it out before you move in any closer."

Arnold Primm waved confirmation from the driver's

seat. Beside him, Todd Mulaney reined the team to a standstill, some thirty yards out from the burned zone.

"I'm not looking forward to this one damn bit," Ruggles told Thorn.

"You knew them well?" asked Gideon.

"We might have passed a dozen words between us in a given year before the Conyers raid. But still..."

Thorn nodded. Said, "You want me to, I can ride in and have the first look unofficially."

"Nope," Ruggles replied. "It's still my job."

"Outside your jurisdiction, though."

"Guess I'm the next best thing until the sheriff's office finally wakes up."

"Okay, then. After you," Thorn said.

In fact, he only lagged a yard or so behind the marshal's bay as they approached the bleak remains of an established home and ranch. Ruggles saw half a dozen chickens running loose around the farmyard, seemingly the only livestock that had managed to escape the barn before its flaming room caved in. He blotted out the mental image of the Fletchers and their boys beneath those piles of ash. For now, the suffering of helpless beasts was all his mind could handle, even knowing that was not the worst of what still lay in store for him today.

He urged the bay mare forward, turning from the house, whose chimney had collapsed during the blaze. "I want to check the barn first," he told Thorn.

"Suits me."

Some twenty feet outside the scorched-earth circle of the barn, both men dismounted, left their animals with reins dangling, and closed the gap on foot. They left their pistols holstered, not expecting any challenge from the ashes, but Ruggles released the hammer thong that held his Colt in leather all the same.

"How many head of stock did Fletcher keep?" Thorn asked.

"The last I heard, five or six steers and maybe twice that many sheep" Ruggles replied.

"It doesn't look like any made it out," said Gideon.

"No, it does not." The marshal glowered as he started walking over powdered ash. "I'd give a week's pay just to know what happened here."

Thorn shared the marshal's curiosity about the fire that had consumed the Fletcher homestead. Nothing at the past crime scenes, from what he'd read or seen in person, had approached this level of destruction, even when selected farmers and their stock were torn apart and left to rot.

The remains of last night's fire had cooled enough for them to walk across the ashes, boots sinking an inch or more into the soot and charcoal left by burning timbers as they fell. It took a moment before Thorn could pick out the remains of animals caught in the fire, bones flensed of hide, muscles, and flesh by searing flames. Cow skeletons were larger than the sheep who'd died beside them and were readily identified by horns. Their legs and necks were tense, twisted by their death throes and the encroaching heat that baked them to the bone.

Thorn hated seeing that but knew there would be worse waiting to greet them when they reached the house.

Or sooner yet.

"I've got a person over here," said Ruggles, choking on revulsion. Bending from the waist, he held aloft the remnant of a lever-action rifle with its wooden stock and foregrip burned away. "Looks like a Henry, which should make this Eddie Fletcher."

"No one else?" asked Gideon.

"Not that I've seen so far."

They spent another fifteen minutes treading over ash and bones before they gave it up and walked back to their waiting horses. Ruggles signaled for Primm's wagon to approach, greeting the undertaker with, "One man inside. We're going to the house now."

Thorn and Ruggles led their horses closer to the caved-in former dwelling, stopping near the porch. No walls remained, much less a door, but Gideon still felt as if they ought to knock and ask permission to proceed. Instead, they crossed the cindered porch and moved through space once occupied by rooms that Thorn had never seen on his first visit to the spread.

No animals had lived inside the house. They found one skeleton beside a blackened stove, one foot still wearing what appeared to be a woman's shoe. "Must be Clarice," said Ruggles, pointing toward a pistol balanced on the ribcage, muzzle thrust at a peculiar angle underneath a sagging lower jaw. "Now, what in hell...?"

"You think she took her own life?" Thorn inquired, hating to voice the notion.

"Rather than defend her boys, you mean?" The marshal shook his head, leaving the six-gun where it was. "I wouldn't want to think so, but I've seen too many *loco* things of late to say for sure. If that's the case, I have to wonder—"

"What would frighten her that badly," Thorn finished the lawman's thought for him.

"Exactly. Do you have any ideas?"

Gideon had a growing list in mind, but nothing that he'd faced before quite fit the present circumstances. "I'm still giving it some thought," he said. "Meanwhile, we'd better try to find the boys."

They found them in what once had been a backroom, huddled underneath a scorched bedframe, arms wrapped around each other as the searing heat or something else ended their lives too soon. Thorn told himself their mouths were both agape from having muscles burned away and not from screaming out in mortal terror but he realized it hardly mattered either way.

"More work for Primm," said Ruggles, turning from the grim sight in disgust.

Cha-time, mentally and physically exhausted, slept late on the morning after the attack on Eddie Fletcher's homestead. When he woke at half-past ten a.m., he sat up in his *tipi* with a start, shocking his woman Ahote from sleep.

Ahote's name translated into English meaning "restless one," but on this day, still groggy, she might well have snapped at Cha-time, provoking him to strike her, if she had not seen the dazed expression on her lover's face.

In fact, Cha-time felt as if he had been roused from sleep by someone clutching at his arm, shaking it roughly, but when sitting upright that sensation faded in a heartbeat. Rather, it was relocated to a point inside his head, behind his blinking eyes, as if something or someone were attempting to escape the confines of his skull.

It was a rude awakening and a sensation Cha-time had never felt before, during, or after any of his occult rituals since he'd been working to become a shaman of the Yaqui tribe. It felt as if someone had crawled inside his head while Cha-time was sleeping and was rifling through his mind to track him down.

A soft touch on his arm startled him further, as Ahote's troubled voice addressed him. "What disturbs you?" she asked urgently.

Shaking off her hand, Cha-time bolted to his feet, then lost his balance, nearly toppling into the ashes of a small fire kindled overnight to keep the inside of their *tipi* warm. No longer necessary with the sun climbing an azure sky, the fire's remains were cold now, which reminded Cha-time of flashes from his mental observation of the *diablero*'s rampage miles away. He muttered something, words immediately lost to him, then snapped out of his waking trance by strength of will alone.

Inside Cha-time's head, the presence of an enemy invader rippled, then evaporated and was gone.

Someone of power nearly equal to his own was bent on stopping him before his plan for ridding Pima County of its European plague was carried to fruition. If Cha-time was not cautious now, prepared to strike directly at his unknown foe...

Snarling, he bolted past Ahote, nearly stepping on her, pushing through the *tipi*'s flap and rushing toward a second tent no more than twenty paces from his own.

"Chu'a!" he shouted, almost literally loud enough to wake the dead. "Get up! There's no more time for sleeping now!"

On their ride back into Hades, Thorn briefed Marshal

Ruggles on his visit from the old Yaqui Hania at the Commodore Hotel.

"You didn't think to mention this before?" the lawman asked.

"I thought about it, sure," said Gideon, "but didn't know if I could credit it. Still don't, in fact."

"Okay, I see your point," Ruggles allowed. "It could be nothing. Likely *is* nothing. I wouldn't want it getting out and stirring people up more than they are already."

"And Hania?" Thorn pressed. "Do you know him?"

"Never heard of him but that's no big surprise," the lawman answered back. "Contact between the Yaquis and the Hades townsfolk don't go much beyond trading supplies from time to time. The tribesmen don't buy much, considering most of them haven't got two cents to rub together. Whites look down on them, of course, Mexicans too. I can't imagine that the Yaquis give a damn whether we live or die but it's been years since there was any kind of real hostility. You know, the killing kind."

Thorn knew the kind, all right. He'd seen it in all colors as he traveled through the West and Border South, In Arkansas, where Dina Pilcher nearly lost her life and soul, racism had been spiked with voodoo lifted from its distant home in Africa, twisted by avaricious hands during its transit to Louisiana's bayous via the Caribbean. In Mississippi, he had seen the scars of chattel slavery laid bare, obstructing his pursuit of a gluttonous monster from the dawn of time.

"You know about the *diablero*?" he asked Ruggles.

"Well, I've *heard* of it, the same as anybody else who's spent time in the territory. Never put much faith in it, myself." The marshal cast a sidelong glance at Gideon, one eyebrow raised. "Do you believe in it?"

"Haven't made up my mind," Thorn said. "I've learned to wait and see on things like that."

"You've run into some things, though, that were... similar?"

"But not the same," amended Gideon. "Not quite. Seems like there's always something new. Or older than the hills."

"I guess the bad news," Ruggles quipped, "is that it wants to kill you."

"Granted, that's a downside," Thorn agreed.

A snort of laughter from the lawman, then he said, "I wouldn't want to trade lives with you. Honestly, what keeps you going at it?"

"Honestly," Gideon answered him, "most days I couldn't rightly say."

HADES

Doc Maddox autopsied the Fletchers in the body-preparation room of Arnold Primm's funeral home, with Primm, Gideon Thorn, and Marshal Ruggles in attendance. Also present, having talked his way in by persuading Ruggles that the Fletchers were parishioners at Mercy Baptist, Pastor Blake stood back and muttered prayers for souls long gone beyond his reach.

"As far as cause of death," Maddox informed his audience, "I can't say absolutely on the man or children. They were obviously burned, the worst I've seen, and Mr. Fletcher's head wounds *might* have happened when the barn caved in on him."

"Might have," Ruggles echoed. "But you're not sure?"

"There's too much damage from the fire for any positive conclusion. Same thing with the two boys. They were underneath a bed, you say?"

"Like they were hiding," Ruggles said.

A moan escaped from Pastor Blake before he launched into another round of whispered prayers. "Our father..."

"What about the woman," Thorn inquired. "The way we found her pistol..."

"It's entirely possible she shot herself," Maddox replied. "Some people do that, obviously, when confronted by a fear that snaps their minds, but with her children to protect, I just can't say. She *is* missing a chunk of her parietal bone—that's the upper portion of her skull between the coronal and the lambdoid sutures, here—" pointing, adding, "but once again, a roof caved in on her and we don't have the full skull for examination. It's a toss-up, gentlemen."

"Closed caskets, any way you slice it," Arnold Primm observed.

Ruggles half turned toward Blake, to interrupt his singsong praying. "Pastor," he inquired, "did they have any next of kin?"

Startled out of his private thoughts, Blake met the lawman's gaze and shook his head. "They came on Sundays, once or twice a month as work allowed, and to an Easter ceremony I recall. We never spoke about extended family."

"So, there's no one to notify. Ellis will have a story in the *Flame,* of course. If it's picked up in Tucson or in Phoenix, word may reach whatever relatives they may have had."

"I'll get the word out to some of my colleagues," Primm advised. "Fletcher's a fairly common name but they can ask around."

"Thanks, Arnold," Ruggles said. "Whatever anyone can

do might help. Meanwhile, with nothing left behind to foot the bill for burying..."

He let it go at that, Primm nodding in acceptance that he likely wouldn't see a dime for any of his work on four more funerals.

"This needs to stop," Julius Maddox said to no one in particular.

"We're working on it, Doc," Ruggles assured him, "but for now, if I made any promises, I'd just be blowing smoke."

The impact of his words caught up with Ruggles even as they left his lips and forced a strangled kind of laughter from his throat. He caught Thorn smiling ruefully, Maddox and Primm shaking their heads, while Pastor Blake stood back and looked aghast.

We're whistling past the graveyard, Ruggles thought.

And wondered to himself who'd be the next one going underground.

ELEVEN

MERCY BAPTIST CHURCH, HADES

Gideon Thorn sat in the back row of the chapel beside Marshal Ruggles, keeping east access to the only exit visible. Both men had doffed their hats on entering, Thorn's balanced on his lap, while locals who had not seen him in either restaurant before got their first glimpse of the white blaze that ran along the central part of his black hair.

Reverend Blake had called the special gathering after attending the autopsies carried out at Arnold Primm's funeral parlor. He had left the undertaker's backroom looking pale and shaken, older than his years, but, as he took the pulpit now, Thorn saw that Blake had managed to recover from that trauma more or less, his face and manner stoked with obvious desire to preach.

And to collect more offerings before the normal Sunday services, Gideon thought.

If that seemed cynical, he'd been around enough to know that it was also likely true.

Blake cleared his throat and then began to preach.

"My friends," he told his audience, "the Devil walks among us in these troubled times. I don't mean ordinary sin, mind you, the things that lead us all astray since Eve spoke honeyed lies to Adam in the garden, long ago. I mean exactly what I say this evening. The Devil! Satan in the flesh, people, as he has not appeared on Earth since Christ Almighty spent his forty days and nights in the Judaean Desert, tempted in such ways as no man since has ever faced! He walks among us, neighbors, and he's reaping bodies right along with souls!"

The crowd was murmuring, a couple of its older members shouting out, "Amen!" Ruggles leaned close to Gideon and whispered, "Has he lost his mind?"

Thorn shrugged and waited for the pastor to continue, knowing there was more to come.

"But this time, children," Blake pressed on, his volume rising, "Satan had a *tribe*. He's not alone in visiting our small Christian community with blood and pain!"

Gideon could have asked what Christian settlement chose Hades as its name but held his tongue.

"And Satan's tribe in Pima County has a name," Blake told his gathered congregants. "You know it, friends. You do! Dirt-worshipers who bow and scrape to heathen gods and demons, showing no regard for Christ Our King! Some of us knew this time would come. It was predictable from Revelation's portrait of the final days! Their name is *Yaqui* and they stand before us on the field of Armageddon, armed for battle as it was foretold in scripture!"

Half the crowd or more was snarling now, some of its members shouting out agreement with Blake's message. Someone near the front row half-rose to his feet, waving a fist aloft, and called out, "Beat 'em to it!"

"Yes!" Blake crowed, rounding the podium, both fists

raise toward the chapel's rafters. "If the Day of Judgment is upon us, we must not present ourselves as lambs to slaughter but, as men and women of the Lord, prepared to fight and win!"

"For God's sake," Ruggles muttered, on his feet now, pushing past Thorn to the church's central aisle. "This has gone far enough!"

Bret Ruggles donned his hat, rested his right hand on his holstered Colt, and shouted down the room toward Blake.

"Hold on there, Reverend! There's absolutely nothing to connect the Yaquis or their reservation with what's happened for the past two months in Pima County and you know it. Whatever you may think about the situation, everybody here knows that inciting violence is a crime."

Blake's congregants had turned to gape at Ruggles now, as if he had two heads or had walked in yelling some language none of them could understand. A couple of the farmers seated farthest from him in the chapel hollered back and shook their fists. One in particular cried out, "What law are you defending, Marshal? God's or man's?"

Another rose and challenged Ruggles, "What have *you* done during all these killings? Anything, besides go out and haul the bodies back to town?"

Ruggles called his accuser out by name. "Sam Jackson, you were on the city council some years back. You know as well as I do that I've got no jurisdiction once I step outside of Hades."

"Nothing but excuses!" Jackson bellowed at him. "If we had a lawman worth his salt—"

"Shut up and listen for a minute!" Ruggles ordered.

"Everybody here knows that the Pima County sheriff's office hasn't done a thing to help us out so far. I've got a stack of telegrams claiming they're understaffed and underfunded, busy chasing rustlers on the big ranches around Tucson. You want to hear excuse, take a look at those. I'll have them printed in the *Flame if* you won't take my word for it."

Another man stood up then, saying, "We don't care about the sheriff. It's another three years yet, before we get to vote him out. We need real help right now!"

"All right," said Ruggles, speaking to the crowd at large. "Which one of you will tell me what I should be doing that I haven't done already? Anyone? Speak up and don't be shy!"

Reverend Blake hammered his pulpit with a clenched fist, shouting down the room, "I've answered that already, Marshal. We must drive the filthy Yaquis from our midst before their devil-worship dooms us all!"

"It hasn't been five minutes since you claimed they worship dirt," Ruggles replied. "Which is it, Pastor? Can't you keep your stories straight?"

At that, the audience began to boo at Ruggles. He considered squeezing off a shot into the chapel's ceiling but decided that would only drive them wild—or wilder, as the case might be. Instead, he answered back to all and sundry, "Anyone who tries to trespass on the reservation can expect to be arrested. Travel armed and it might turn out even worse for you. Expect no second warning, people."

Ruggles had a glimpse of Thorn rising to follow him as he stormed out, moving with long strides toward his office.

"What's the next move?" Gideon called after him.

Not turning, Ruggles said over his shoulder, "Next, I need to find some deputies."

WEST OF HADES

Hania was roasting rabbit for his lunch, a small one, when a wave of sudden nausea swept over him. He recognized the feeling, understood that it meant trouble was on the way, but was surprised to feel it split this time, tugging his mind and gut in different directions simultaneously.

Some of that sensation radiated from the town whose settlers called it Hades in perverse defiance of their Holy Bible's cursed Hell. The rest drew Hania's attention toward the northwest of his humble camp, where he could feel a ritual in progress, summoning a *diablero* to defend his fellow tribesmen on the Yaqui reservation from whatever violence inhabitants of Hades were debating at that hour.

Hania was not officially a member of the reservation's tribe. Years had elapsed since he had pitched his *tipi* on the land decreed as safe for Yaquis within Arizona Territory. Confident that no one from his tribe has missed him in the interim, the shaman lived alone and made his own way in the world, fair game for anyone who happened by and took offense to his inhabiting the open desert. Someday, he realized, that independence might well be the death of him, with no white lawman troubled by his passing in the least, but Hania had long since made his peace with death.

It held no terrors for him though, if he were honest with himself, he feared the *diablero* and its master to his very core.

Forgetting hunger, Hania decided to sort out the feelings that had come upon him unaware. The turmoil flaring up in Hades was no mystery. Its people, terrified by weeks of grisly death, were arming to react in a misguided bid to halt the evil at its source. That source, in turn—still unidentified by Hania—was making ready to respond in kind with bloodletting beyond what Pima County had experienced so far.

And if that happened, Hania determined from the roiling in his gut, it could mean all-out war.

HADES

As Thorn approached the marshal's office, Winchester tucked underneath one arm, Bert Ruggles stepped onto the sidewalk, saw him, and called out, "This isn't your fight, Gideon."

"You're good for deputies, I take it?" Thorn inquired.

"Not so you'd notice," Ruggles said. "So far, it's Todd Mulaney."

"That kid from the undertaker's shop?"

"I know," the lawman said. "But he's an orphan, game for anything, and everybody else in town is either scared of Pastor Connor or just scared to death in general. The ones riding with Connor reckon nothing else will stop these killings. I expect the rest will be inside behind locked doors, waiting to find out if their neighbors win the day or tribesmen mad as wet hens show up hunting scalps."

"I'd hate to bet on either side," said Gideon.

"Seems like the end of Hades, either way," Ruggles replied. "The end for me, at least."

"You're pulling out?"

"I'll see this through," the marshal said. "If I come out the other side of it alive, I'm done trying to hold this town in line. It's just a mob now, with some quitters ready to throw in the towel."

"They'll need a strong hand all the more," said Gideon.

"Then let them find another one. Somebody they'll respect. Smart money says there won't be many takers after this."

"You're set on riding with Mulaney?"

"Hate to do it," Ruggles said, "but he's a crack shot, even if he's never drawn down on a man."

"He's waiting for us at the livery?"

"I'm on my way down there right now. Connor and his gang have a short head start on us."

"Okay," said Thorn. "I guess we shouldn't keep them waiting then."

Not for the first time, he was glad that Dinah Pilcher was at home in Boston, safe and sound. That image made Gideon wonder whether they would ever meet again.

NORTHWEST OF HADES

Cha-time knelt beside Chu'a, watching the rise and shimmer into physical existence from the colored flames of his campfire. Chanting the prayers that would embolden it to follow his instructions, he wondered if it could face and overcome the fury rising out of Hades from the white minister's house of worship.

Cha-time believed that it was equal to the task. If not entirely, it could still strike fear into the settlers' hearts and souls. If they were somehow able to defeat the shaman's proud creation, at the very least, they would be taught a lesson in humility.

And Cha-time could always try again.

He thought about his people on the Yaqui reservation, unaware that they might soon be set upon by white men in a lynching mood. The shaman felt ambiguous about that danger, knowing he had prompted the attack with his attempts to help his fellow tribesmen, but he still saw no alternative to the course he had set two months ago.

This was his moment. Cha-time could no more take it back than he snatch an errant thought out of the air and stuff it back inside his brain.

As for Chu'a, what of him? Should Cha-time fall in battle, his assistant knew the proper spells and incantations to evoke another *diablero* from the Other Side and set it free upon the trespassers in Arizona Territory. If he lacked the courage to pursues that course alone, Cha-time would not be around to watch him fail.

In front of them, the *diablero* stepped clear of its birthing fire and spread its mighty arms as if to clasp the shades of dusk that stained the desert gray and purple on the verge of night.

The mob from Hades had been foolish, setting off from town late in the afternoon. Full dark might fall upon them before they crossed over to the Yaqui reservation, past the U.S. Army's warning signs that they had entered Native land.

No matter.

Cha-time had sharp eyes, day or night, and the demon that he had conjured saw in multiple dimensions. It was bulletproof, impervious to fire, and could not be destroyed by any weapon in the white man's puny arsenal.

Only another shaman could defeat it and, if such a one existed, he would have to overcome Cha-time first.

The odds against that, Cha-time decided, were extreme.

Riding out of Hades with three dozen townsmen, Connor Blake felt confident that he had made the right decision for his people and their God. How many times in scripture had the Lord dispatched his chosen nations into battle against heathens sworn to serve the cause of other gods?

Each time, although outnumbered on the field, God's people had emerged victorious. Blake trusted that because the Holy Bible told him so and who dared contradict God's word?

With that in mind, the minister had brought no weapons other than the Bible with him as he left town, riding in the forefront of his righteous posse to avenge the wrongs that had been done to his little community. In fact, Blake *owned* no weapons other than some kitchen knives he used in preparation of his solitary meals around the parsonage because, until this day, he'd always thought himself a man of peace.

But that went out the window when the Devil came to town and started reaping souls.

Jolting across the open desert on his brindle mare, no horseman worthy of the name, Blake thought about the man in black—Gideon Thorn—who'd visited his church that afternoon and left with Marshal Ruggles when the lawman interrupted Blake's oration to his flock. There was something about the drifter, said to be experienced in matters of an occult nature, that disturbed Reverend Blake.

Was he another of the Devil's emissaries in their midst, arriving as he had around the same time slaughter in the neighborhood of Hades had advanced from animals to settlers? Could he be a demon cast in human form, sent to exacerbate the fear that had enveloped Hades since July?

The guns Thorn wore, presumably, were not for show alone but he and Marshal Ruggles could not stand against the thirty-odd parishioners riding with Blake against the heathen Yaquis. Even if Blake could believe the rumors that the undertaker's young apprentice had agreed to join them, Todd Mulaney scarcely counted. He was just a child, easily swayed and led astray.

If he opposed God's messengers, he would be trampled underfoot.

No one could stand before the righteous power of the Lord, a mighty man of war as He proclaimed himself in Exodus, Chapter 15.

Tonight was bound to be a victory, whether or not Blake lived to tell the tale next Sunday morning from the dais of his humble church.

His name would be remembered in the streets of Hades, come what may.

Hania tracked the *diablero* with his mind, felt it advancing toward the Yaqui reservation, and was momentarily confused.

Why would the demon's master send it off in that direction rather than selecting other settlers' homesteads for attack? A moment later, his thoughts clarified, awash with images of a white mob riding from Hades to the rez, led by the town's appointed holy man from Mercy Baptist Church. Something had snapped after the *diablero*'s last attack and set the townsfolk on a warpath of their own.

What could Hania do about it?

He had no firm fix on the mob's location, changing by the moment as it covered ground but, from the feelings he experienced, Hania knew it must be separated from his camp by six or seven miles at least. He could be up and moving on his unshod Appaloosa pony within ten to fifteen minutes but the mob could likely reach the reservation in that time.

Or if the *diablero* had its marching orders from the Yaqui who controlled it, they might meet disaster on the road.

Hania felt no sympathy for anyone who tried to do his people harm, whether their acts were spurred by racial hatred or, as in the case of whoever controlled the *diablero*, meant to "help" the tribe wreaking terror. That terror would ultimately end with U.S. troops dispatched from Fort Grant or Camp Ord to quell the violence. A wise man should have known Yaquis could only lose in that scenario —although the cavalry, in past campaigns, has never faced a *diablero* on a rampage.

Hania thought it might be interesting, watching that play out, but he was honor bound to head off any lethal violence within the limitations of his power.

Rising on stiffened legs, the shaman gathered he belongings and prepared to ride. If nothing else, he might arrive in time to gain some knowledge as to where the *diablero* was dispatched from and which Yaqui shaman was responsible. And after that...?

But first things first.

Intruding on what had the makings of a riot or an outright massacre, Hania knew his first concern lay with not being one of those who fell upon the battlefield. Dead, he could not help anyone and it would be no consolation if his spirit found the answers he was seeking on the Other Side where he could take no action on the earthly plane.

Resolved to do whatever might be possible within his

limitations, Hania mounted his Appaloosa and set off to the northeast.

"How far off is the Yaqui reservation," Thorn asked Marshal Ruggles, riding to his left. Young Todd Mulaney trailed them by a few yards as if feeling out of place with two armed older men now that they'd put Hades behind them and were riding over open desert.

"Eight, maybe nine miles from where we are right now," Ruggles replied. "Blake and his so-called posse have a lead on us but I'm still hoping we can make it up."

"Who has authority over the reservation?" Thorn inquired.

"Not me," the lawman answered ruefully. "Reservations are administered by the Bureau of Indian Affairs, attached to the to the U.S. War Department from 1832 to '49, switched over to the Interior Department from there. If there's a problem, someone wires the U.S. Marshal based in Phoenix and he sends a deputy to nose around if he's concerned enough about it."

"And who would send that wire?" asked Gideon.

"Should be the county sheriff but he's dropped the ball on this mess since day one. Mind you, until Blake started spouting off about the Yaquis, there's been nothing to connect them with the killings."

"And now Blake is on the verge of starting up a war," Thorn said.

"I doubt he sees it that way," Ruggles answered back. "When he gets fired up on his scripture, everything turns black and white. A few years back he tried to close The Prairie Dog and Diamond Lil's for peddling booze and women but his congregation withered to a handful in a month or so, with most of those who stayed on being housewives and their kids. No money in it for a preacher from that bunch, so he laid off but never got a full house back until the killings started in July."

One thing that Gideon had never liked about traditional preachers was how they battened onto handy causes, shifting as the wind changed, one eye always on the flow of tithes and offerings. He'd never met a one who followed Christ's command from Luke Chapter 18: "Sell all that thou hast and distribute unto the poor and come follow me."

Back east, some preachers lived in splendor rivaling the dukes and kings of old, preaching in churches that resembled art museums, with fortunes banked away, and couldn't find the nearest slum without a guide.

Thorn guessed that they had ridden for another mile or so, approximately, when reports of gunfire carried on the desert wind informed him they were probably too late.

TWELVE

NORTHWEST OF HADES

Reverend Connor Blake was not accustomed to long rides around the countryside but kept his brindle mare, a gift from one of his parishioners, for those occasions when he visited an ailing member of his congregation on some nearby farm. This evening, the gallop out from town had jolted him and made the pastor wish that he could turn toward home but he had shut that door and locked it tight against himself.

Now there was nothing he could do but forge ahead and carry out the half-baked scheme he had devised while railing his angry, frightened fellow townsmen.

And second thoughts were nagging at him, telling Blake that he, just possibly, had been a fool, betrayed by pride, one of the seven deadly sins.

In fact, Saint Augustine had called pride the first sin, which had betrayed Satan himself into rebellion and resulted in his fall from grace, along with other foolish angels who had followed him. It prompted even righteous men to boast, best, and belittle other humans no more prone to weakness or transgression than themselves.

Today, Blake wondered if his pride might land him in a prison cell—or worse if it might get him killed.

The minister had never been a fighting man, although his calling predisposed him to an endless war with evil. Now, having recruited followers through rhetoric alone, he was compelled to follow up and see the matter through.

But Lord, he missed his parsonage in town.

At first, Blake thought his aged eyes were playing tricks on him as dusk descended but he wiped them with a rough swipe of his hand and nothing changed. Some distance up ahead, a man had suddenly appeared directly in the middle of the desert trail Blake and his riders had been following from Hades toward the Yaquis reservation, standing fast it seemed, as if to block their path.

But no. As seconds passed Blake realized it could not be a normal man. It had been hiding somehow, standing tall beside a Joshua tree, and *tall* would be the operative word. Unless Blake missed his guess, the tree was nine or ten feet tall, and yet the figure next to it seemed close to the same height.

Impossible!

Blake knew his mind must be deceiving him—or hoped so, until one of his companions on the ride called out behind him, "What in Hell is that?"

Blake winced at the profanity but could not fault the sentiment.

Unless the sudden churning in his gut deceived him, Hell indeed might not be far away.

The first gunshot, a rifle, sounded like the distant cracking of a bullwhip, audible but near impossible to pinpoint. When the firing turned into a flurry, Thorn asked Marshal Ruggles, "How much farther to the Yaqui reservation?"

"Too far off for shooting to sound that close," Ruggles said.

"What's your next best guess, then?" Gideon inquired.

"I haven't got a clue. Blake's men ran into trouble but, beyond that, your guess is as good as mine."

"We'd better check it out then," Thorn suggested.

"Right." Before proceeding, Ruggles turned to their companion. Said, "That sounds like more grief than you bargained for, Todd. No shame in it if you need to turn around."

"I volunteered," Mulaney said. "I'm sticking with it, Marshal."

"Fair enough, then," Ruggles said. "Let's ride!"

Thorn knew that Connor Blake had taken close to twenty townsmen with him on their foray to the reservation and it sounded as if all of them were firing guns now, somewhere up ahead a mile or so. He wore no spurs when riding Shadow, knew a nudge would do the trick, and Gideon was ready as his stallion bolted forward, homing on the sounds of battle like a proper warhorse.

Gideon, for his part, wondered if that was a terrible idea.

Raising the subject now might make the lawman think he was deranged and all the more so if they found no sign of any demon at their journey's end. It was as likely, Thorn supposed, that warriors from the Yaqui reservation had detected the approach by hostile whites and ridden out to meet them where no peril would endanger any innocents.

But, on the other hand...

When they were still three hundred yards or so out from the swirling battleground, Thorn glimpsed a figure twice as large as any normal man moving among the rearing horses and their fallen riders. He attempted to dismiss it as a trick of light, dusk closing in upon them rapidly, but then the giant literally tossed a horse aside, its legs flailing in panic, rider spilling from his saddle with a strangled cry.

Behind him, Todd Mulvaney cursed. Brett Ruggles asked, "What am I looking at, for God's sake?"

"I'm not sure," said Gideon, wishing it didn't feel like he was lying. "First, we need to find out if it's bulletproof."

The *diablero* felt exhilarated as it always did when slaughtering its enemies. Their puny weapons had no more effect upon it than a gnat's bite on a bison's hide, if any of that noble species still survived the white man's ruthless war on nature.

Killing was the *diablero*'s sole reason for living—what the *Mexicanos* called *razón para vivir*—once it was summoned by its human master from the Other Side. It recognized the difference between Natives and Outsiders but was not always scrupulous about persons it eliminated and the ones it spared.

In fact, if called up by a Yaqui, it was not averse to slaying Mescaleros, Navajos, Comanches, take your pick. In wartime between tribes, it served whoever called it forth and set it on the path toward blood and carnage.

Under certain circumstances, it could even turn upon its earthly master and, while that had crossed its demon's mind of late, it still had labors to complete before a break was made, letting it roam abroad at will by day or night.

Not yet.

For now, it was enough to rush among the frightened riders who had meant to storm the Yaqui reservation. Their pathetic leader was a holy man of sorts whose courage had deserted him the moment that he glimpsed the *diablero* in its almost-flesh, able to rip and render enemies with fang and claw while still impervious to pellets from their useless firearms.

A panicked mare rushed toward it now, then recognized its grim mistake too late. Rearing, the horse flailed with its forehooves, all that it could manage in a vain attempt to save itself from slaughter as the *diablero* moved in close and swung one might hand with taloned fingers flexed. Its claws sheared through the horse's throat latch like exaggerated razor blades, released a flood of crimson from its severed arteries and veins.

The *diablero* caught some of that blood in its mouth, from the air, and gulped it down, watching the animal before it fall into its death throes. Trapped beneath it, one foot still inside a stirrup, its doomed rider shrieked in agony as his mount, weighing nearly half a ton, rolled over him, crushing his pelvis and the organs it contained.

To silence him, the *diablero* stooped and flicked one hand across his throat, releasing more sweet blood onto the arid desert soil. At the same time, half of the horseman's screaming face tore free and rolled up toward his forehead like a window shade.

The shrieking ceased, while other riders cursed or shouted imprecations to their god, firing their weapons with a frenzied haste that sent half of their bullets whining into empty space. Those who did better left no marks upon the *diablero* and it felt nothing from their futile attempts to bring it down.

Without the proper incantations from its master or another shaman, no tool forged by men could stop the *diablero* once its marching orders were received.

Until its designated targets were eliminated root and branch.

Snarling, it swept on through the other riders, slashing to its left and right in turn, pausing to snatch one rider from his saddle, rip into his throat with avid jaws, and gulp life by the quart as it poured out of him.

Waste not, want not.

Hania sat astride his Appaloosa pony, half a mile distant from the ongoing massacre, eyes narrowed in the failing light as he watched white men and their horses die.

He felt bad for the horses, nothing for the men whose race had hounded his to near extinction for the best part of three hundred fifty years. Hania would not miss them, although neither did he think the world would be greatly improved by their removal from it.

Their ancestors had inflicted too much damage, as it was, for that to be reversed until more centuries had passed —and even that might not time enough.

Above all, Hania experienced a sense of failure, feeling that he should have found some way to stop the *diablero* before it could wreak such havoc on the land. Unfortunately, that could only be achieved by taking out the shaman who had summoned it initially and while Hania had a fair idea of his identity, that was a far cry from locating where he stayed and worked his magic.

And now, distracting him, Hania felt more riders drawing near as if to join the fight. Although beyond his line of sight as yet, the old man sensed that one of them possessed an aura he had glimpsed before, the man in black he had confronted at the Continental Hotel earlier.

Gideon Thorn.

The hunter's two companions, Hania intuited, were the lawman from Hades and a youngster he could not identify, foolish enough to join in hunting down a *diablero* when his party had no chance of stopping it.

For that, they would require advice and the ability to take it, two distinctly different things and traits which few white men possessed in dealings with a lowly "Indian." Soon, they would glimpse the *diablero* slaughtering the marshal's citizens and, if it did not butcher them with all the rest, then Thorn, at least, might be amenable to listening and learning.

Might absorb what was required to end the demon's rampage.

And it not...well, then, Hania would be forced to manage it himself or sacrifice his own life trying.

"Hold up right here!" Thorn called to his companions and all three reined in.

"What is it?" Ruggles asked. "Why are we hanging back?"

"See for yourself," Thorn answered, nodding toward the fight in progress.

He had noted that the guns carried by Connor Blake's

raiders seemed to be having no effect upon the massive figure at the center of the brutal action up ahead. Whatever it might be, whether composed of flesh and blood or something else entirely, never mind how frightened the collected Hades townsmen were, at least a few of them must have scored close-range hits by now but none of their rounds slowed the enemy a bit, much less debilitating it.

Young Todd Mulaney saw it next, blurting, "Their shots ain't getting through."

"So, what?" the marshal challenged his companions. "Did we ride out here to sit and watch that thing, whatever it is, kill a quarter of the men in town?"

"I'll tell you what I didn't do," Thorn answered back. "That's make the trip to wind up dead without a fighting chance."

"Okay, so do you have a better plan?" asked Ruggles.

"Not off-hand," Gideon granted ruefully. "I've seen enough to know that charging in with all guns blazing is a waste of time."

"Jesus!" The marshal's face had paled despite dusk's shadows closing in. "To just hang back and watch this..."

Raw emotion choked him for a moment. Thorn waited it out, then asked, "What have you heard about the *diablero*?"

Ruggles looked at him askance. "You're serious?"

Thorn nodded toward the fight before them, swirling dust and tumbling bodies all around, a giant moving in its midst. "What do you think?" he answered.

"It's some kind of Native superstition. I've heard different versions of it over time. Some say the *diablero* is a shaman who can change into a bird, coyote, or some other animal. Another story makes it out to be a demon. Not the straight-up Devil, which would be *diablo,* but one of the Devil's helpers, lackies, call it whatever you like."

"The second one," Thorn narrowed down his question. "Have you heard that shamans with a special gift can summon it to life on Earth?"

"Come on, now!" Ruggles fairly scoffed. "You think *that* came from Hell because some crazy person called it out?"

"I never mentioned crazy," Gideon replied, "since that would make the person wrong. But would you say that what we're seeing is a man, just overgrown somehow? Somebody like that giant P. T. Barnum's sideshow used to have beside the dog-faced boy and bearded lady back before the place burned down?"

Ruggles considered that, but briefly. "No," he said. "If that's a man, I've never heard of anybody like it. And the way it's killing people, *biting* some of them...I just don't know."

"A Yaqui came to see me at the Continental," Gideon disclosed, "and told me that a shaman from his tribe had raised a *diablero* right around the time our killings started."

"But you didn't think to tell me until now?" the marshal asked.

"I couldn't trust his word alone," Thorn said. "But now...I've got no other explanation for the evidence before my eyes. Do you?"

"Damn it to Hell!" The marshal leaned out from his saddle, spat in anger, but did not ride forward to attack. "So, what do we do now?"

Connor Blake believed his life was over when the giant thing rushed at his brindle mare and clutched its neck, twisting until the horse was lifted skyward, pitching Blake out of his saddle to the ground below.

He'd always thought it was a myth but moments from his past *did* flash behind his eyes, leaving the reverend to wonder if his whole existence had been nothing but a futile span of wasted years—no wife, no children, no sincere fulfillment in his calling until this, his dying day.

A sudden shower, shocking in its warmth, snapped Blake out of his reverie. He sat bolt upright, realizing in a heartbeat that the outpouring was blood from his animal's neck, the beast still held above him in its slayer's grasp. When something landed on the desert floor between his feet, Blake gaped at it and recognized the brindle's severed head, wrenched from the animal by pure brute force.

In that instant, the pastor realized he'd lost his rifle when he fell. Control of his bodily functions followed a heartbeat later and he shamed himself during the final seconds of existence, hot tears streaming down his weathered cheeks.

He heard a snarling sound above him, like a growl of distant thunder, and looked up to find the monster staring down at him with glowing eyes, Blake's mutilated mare held overhead by sinew-bulging arms. He saw bullets striking the supernatural impossibility, rippling its simple buckskin garb, and passing through its flesh—if flesh it was, in fact—with no result.

Another snarl, louder this time, more *personal,* and Pastor Blake watched wide-eyed, screaming, as the creature hurled his horse's carcass down upon him from on high, its body blotting out his last view of the living world.

"What's that?"

Brett Ruggles knew Gideon Thorn had spoken to him but had failed to grasp the meaning of his words, caught up in gaping at the slaughter going on a hundred yards in front of them. He glanced across at Thorn, saw Todd Mulaney weeping, head bowed to shut out the hellish vision.

"I said we need to back away from here," repeated Thorn.

That went against the lawman's grain but he had ruefully acknowledged impotence while watching as the nine-or-ten-foot monster tore apart some of his jurisdiction's leading citizens. The thought that crossed his mind then—*Anyway, I warned them*—felt unworthy, even shameful, piercing Ruggles with a stab of guilt.

The flip side of that coin was understanding that he'd sworn an oath to guard the streets of Hades but had no authority outside its limits. As to his responsibility...well, he would have to ponder that on sleepless nights to come.

Assuming he survived this one.

"Back away and then do what?" he challenged Thorn.

"Find the old Yaqui, calls himself Hania," Gideon replied. "Or hope that he finds me."

"And then?"

"He had the problem figured out before he came to see me last time," Thorn said. "If we're lucky, he may have some kind of a solution figured out."

"And if he doesn't? If you never hear from him again?"

"I'll have to find the shaman who's behind this on my own, somehow, and make him stop."

"Simple," said Ruggles. "Just like that?"

"It won't be simple," Thorn replied, "or strictly legal, either I'm afraid."

"To Hell with legal," Ruggles said. "I'm watching Hades

die in front of me and can't do anything about it. Whatever it takes to stop a repetition of this massacre, I'm there."

That said, with Todd Mulaney still in tears, the trio turned their restless horses back toward town and closed their ears to dwindling screams.

Thorn did not speak again until he calculated they were halfway back to town. Breaking the silence then, he said, "First thing, we need to put the undertaker on alert but hold him back from riding out until daylight."

"You mean to leave the bodies out all night?" asked Ruggles, sounding horrified.

"A few of them may slip away," said Gideon, although he doubted that were true. "From what I've seen, and you've explained about the other death scenes, scavengers won't be a problem."

"Christ! It's come to this, then," Ruggles muttered. "Nothing left to do but dig a bunch more graves."

Beside them, Todd Mulaney spoke up for the first time since they'd come across the desert fight in progress. "Mister Primm has only got the one wagon, you know? Bringing those men back into town, what's left of them, could take all day tomorrow. Making caskets, all of that...I hate to think about it."

"We'll get some kind of work party to help," the lawman said. "Which means my real first job is telling everyone in town their friends, neighbors, and husbands won't be coming home alive."

Thorn began to say, "If you need any help with that—" but Ruggles stopped him short.

"You'd best stay out of it," he said. "Some of the ones

who stayed behind may end up blaming you. I've got no choice but talking to them. You'll be better off in your hotel room while I get through that."

"Whatever you think best," Thorn granted. "Anyway, the Continental's where Hania found me last time."

"If he shows his face again, don't let him get away," Ruggles advised.

"Does that make me a deputy empowered to arrest him?" Gideon inquired.

The marshal made a sour face. Said, "Just ask him to hang around until I have a chance to see him, then. I need to hear his story for myself."

"And you'll believe it?"

"I can't promise that but, after what we've seen, I'll definitely listen to him."

Listening was part of it, all right. But once Ruggles had heard it all and understood the probable prescription for elimination of his problem, would he—*could* he—follow through.

It would mean killing, almost certainly outside his jurisdiction and outside the law.

Thorn would not balk at that but Ruggles wore a badge, followed a certain code of conduct he might not be willing to discard.

And hesitation at a crucial instant might be all it would take to end his life.

THIRTEEN

THE CONTINENTAL HOTEL

Full dark had fallen over Hades as Thorn, Marshal Ruggles, and Todd Mulaney made their way down Easy Street. Thorn and Mulaney stopped off at the livery to bed their horses down while Ruggles moved on toward his office through the shadows cast by its irregular streetlamps.

When Thorn was finished brushing Shadow and communing silently with Belle, he left the stable to discover townsfolk milling in the street. Ruggles was still aboard his mount, scanning the crowd as members of it shouted questions at him, talking over one another in their hunger for an explanation as to what was happening.

Thorn crossed the street, avoiding them, and only two or three of those assembled seemed to note his passing down the opposite sidewalk. The ones who saw him quickly turned their backs, returning their attention to the marshal as he finally dismounted, stepped onto the sidewalk, and began to speak.

"All of you simmer down," he urged. "I can't hear all of

you at once, but if you'll let me get a word in edgeways maybe I can clear things up and let you get back to your homes."

More shouted questions quickly drowned him out.

"Where's Pastor Blake?"

"What's happened to my husband?"

"Did they find the Yaquis?"

"Have you seen them, Marshal?"

Finally, when Thorn was twenty yards or so from his hotel, the lawman drew his Colt, cocked it, and fired it once into the darkened sky. A hush immediately fell over the crowd, although it still remained restless, its members seemingly unable to stand still.

"All right, now. No one say another word until I've finished. If you still have any questions after that, I'll answer them as best I can."

He paused a few more seconds for effect, gun still in hand, then solemnly resumed. "First thing," the lawman said, "we overtook them on the trail. They never made it to the Yaqui reservation."

Breathless muttering resumed but no one dared to interrupt by then.

"Someone or some*thing* intercepted them," Ruggles pressed on. "We couldn't get a clear view of it as the night came on but it was big and ripping through the posse like a house on fire, horses and men alike. That's all I know right now. Can't give you any certain names. I'm hoping some escaped and find their way back home. As for the rest, my next stop after this is Arnold Primm's. We'll head back out there in the morning and retrieve—"

Thorn tuned the rest out as he reached the Continental, knowing there would be no end to questions, accusations, maybe even calls to ride back out tonight and search the battlefield. That would be worse than useless, in his view, certain to get more people killed.

A shadow chose that moment to emerge from hiding in an alley's mouth and block Gideon's path. His hands dropped toward his twin Peacemakers, hesitating as he recognized Hania's form and voice.

"You've seen it, then," the old man said.

"We saw something."

"The *diablero*."

Frowning, Thorn glanced back over his shoulder, faced the shaman once again, and said, "You need to share your story with the marshal."

"And will he believe me now?"

"He'll listen, anyway. I guarantee you that."

Hania nodded. Said, "If you believe it's wise."

"First thing, we need to slip around in back," Thorn said. "These people spot you out here on the street, it just might turn into a necktie party for the two of us."

It took the better part of fifteen minutes for the crowd to finally disperse, men cursing, women sobbing for the menfolk they might never see again. Ruggles advised them all to lock their doors and keep their weapons handy, though he had no reason to believe that either step would keep them safe tonight.

In parting, he had heard a couple of the angry townsfolk mutter, "Coward!" One of them had spat in his direction, then scuttled away before Ruggles could call him on it.

Not that he could argue with their sentiments. Indeed, the marshal had reviled himself in bitter terms throughout the long ride back to town.

Leaving his horse tied to a hitching rail outside the office, Ruggles started on his way toward Primm's funeral home to ruin Arnold's night. Before he covered half that distance, though, a voice called out to him from a dark alleyway between the jail and Harry Delray's hardware store.

Ruggles still had his Colt in hand and cocked it now, turning to face the shadows on his left. "Who's there?" he asked, and followed up with, "Show yourself!"

"Just me," Gideon Thorn replied, emerging. "And I've brought someone to have a word with you."

A shorter man stepped into view, long hair grazing his shoulders, dressed in buckskin, solemn-faced.

"Hey, is that—?"

"Hania," Thorn made the introduction. "He's the Yaqui shaman I was telling you about."

Ruggles half-expected the old native to use sign language. Instead, he simply said, "Marshal, you've seen it now."

"I sure as hell saw something," Ruggles granted. "You claim it's some kind of demon?"

"Called a *diablero*," the Yaqui replied. "And I believe I know which shaman summons it."

"Believing's one thing," Ruggles told him. "Knowing's something else."

"Then let us say I've narrowed down the possibilities to one who has the power and the malice toward your people."

"Has he got a name?" Ruggles inquired.

"Cha-time. His apprentice is a younger man named Chu'a."

"Just like that." The marshal did not try to mask his skepticism. "Can I find them on the rez?"

Hania shook his head, a solid negative. "They are unwelcome there among peace-loving members of the tribe. They live apart and work their medicine away from prying eyes."

"If they're so secretive, how do you know all this?" asked Ruggles.

"When they call the *diablero* forth it leaves...traces. I feel it and can track its movements somewhat as it travels."

"Somewhat. From a feeling."

"He's a shaman, like I told you," Gideon chimed in. "Seems like they're all connected in some kind of way."

"Uh huh." Frowning, still doubtful, Ruggles said, "Okay. Let's step inside and you can lay it out for me."

It was Hania's first time in a lawman's office, noting WANTED posters and a gun rack on the wall. In the back, two jail cells were unoccupied, their iron-barred doors standing ajar.

The marshal sat behind his desk, waved Hania and Thorn to wooden chairs set facing it. "I've got no coffee made," he said. "You'll have to tell the story dry."

"It is a short one," Hania replied. "Cha-time hates all white men, more than most among our tribe. Chu'a wishes to be a shaman in his own right but he lacks the calling from his childhood, serving as *el lacayo* to Cha-time in hopes of learning more."

"*El lacayo,*" Ruggles echoed. "A lackey."

Hania nodded. "I doubt he'd ever have the power to evoke a *diablero* on his own."

"But when he puts his head together with this Cha-time..."

"You have seen the result, I think," said Hania.

"That was a *diablero,* ripping up those men and horses? All the other victims and their animals as well?"

"It can do worse than that," Hania said. "With time and practice, it acquires more power. Already, from what I know, there is only one way to stop it."

Ruggles frowned. Asked, "What would that be?"

"Someone must eliminate the shaman who controls it, Marshal."

"Someone meaning who, exactly?"

"There is no special requirement," Hania replied. "A man or men with courage to confront Cha-time before he can call the *diablero* to defend him."

"You mean kill him."

"Yes. Only that will serve to break his spell."

"You understand that we have laws here in the territory," Ruggles said, not asking him. "I can't just go and kill someone because I feel like it. He has to be arrested, brought to trial and all, or else some judge will wind up hanging me."

"On what charge would he be arrested?" Hania inquired. "Is it a crime under the white man's law to work dark magic? Will a court agree to hear the case? What sentence would apply?"

"Most likely none," Ruggles agreed. "We gave up hunting witches back in 1692 if I recall my history."

"And yet a shaman and his *diablero* kill your people with impunity."

"You say."

Hania nodded. "So ignore the evidence of your own eyes. What will Cha-time do if you arrest him and he's sitting over there?" A gesture toward the empty cells. "What will he do before the trial or during it? While he is locked away in prison, if convicted even on some minor charge?"

"Turn loose this *diablero* thing again, I guess you'll say?"

"In all its fury, Marshal. It is even possible the demon may begin to operate without him, as its power grows."

"Well, first of all, we haven't got a judge in Hades, so I'd have to run him up to court in Tucson. They have a grand jury there, sits once a month, and they'll most likely laugh the whole thing off. Their sheriff blames it all on Mexicans and border trash. He's not likely to change his mind and run a risk of looking foolish in the newspapers."

"In that case," said Hania, "you must either act alone or do nothing. In which case, since the *diablero* has already tasted blood aplenty, there's no reason to believe your town is safe."

Ruggles cursed underneath his breath, then said, "All right. If I agree to this, how would I get it done?"

NORTHWEST OF HADES

Cha-time felt the *diablero* making its way back to his encampment, moving slowly as if sated by its clash with the raiders out of Hades. At the same time, he could sense a difference about the demon he had conjured from Beyond, its blood tingling with energy absorbed from man and horse alike.

And there was something else to which he could not put a name.

"You are concerned, Master," said Chu-a, standing at Cha-time's side.

"Something about our spirit tool has changed," Cha-time said.

"Such as?"

"It is not weary as we might expect after destroying twenty whites or more," Cha-time said. "It feels uneasy. Restless."

"But you can control it still?"

Cha-time nodded but without great confidence. In fact, he was not certain, in that moment, of his power to manipulate the *diablero.* If it had acquired sufficient energy to act without direction from his mind and chanting...

"Here it comes!" Chu'a announced, pointing.

Cha-time saw the looming figure drawing nearer, like a slab of darkness animated, taking on exaggerated human form. It moved with long strides, stout arms swinging at its sides. As it approached the camp, dim firelight showed its face, its massive chest and taloned hands speckled with drying blood.

And it was rumbling in its throat, never a hopeful sign as Cha-time prepared it for another sleep, awaiting his next summons.

When the *diablero* was still thirty yards from camp Cha-time called out to it, "Stop! Advance no further!"

It ignored him, plodding forward, long legs eating up the desert sand. Cha-time saw its fingers flexing as if making ready for a wrestling match, its chest expanding as broad shoulders hunched.

"Stop now!" he cried again. "Your master orders you!"

Instead of halting in its tracks or even slowing down, the *diablero* snarled and grumbled something in an eldritch tongue Cha-time could not translate. Then, as if a leash had been unfastened, it dashed forward in a sprint, directly toward the Yaqui shaman and his ritual assistant, roaring as it came.

"Have you been to this other shaman's camp before?" asked Marshal Ruggles.

"No," Hania said. "In fact, we've never met."

Thorn caught the marshal's sidelong glance and could predict his next inquiry from the wry expression on his face.

"You've never met the man?" Ruggles echoed.

"That's correct," Hania said.

"You seem to know a lot about him for a total stranger," said the lawman. "How's that work."

"Shamans within my tribe are more or less attuned to one another," said Hania. "Then, there is what you might call the process of elimination."

"Come again?"

"To take the second matter first, at any given time the Yaqui have only a given number of shamans. Two of those alive today no longer practice anything but healing medicine and never would have tried to raise a *diablero* even in their younger days. I personally know that *I* am not responsible and that leaves only Cha-time."

"I guess I'll have to take your word on that. But still, how do you know just where to find him."

"When he works his medicine each shaman gives off emanations of his spirit. Others of the same calling can feel it, as you might say, with their hearts and minds. If he projects it long enough, with strength enough, it is as good as any smoke signal."

"And you picked up on this tonight?" asked Ruggles.

"Yes. During the other incidents, I was not certain. Cha-time summoned the *diablero* and dispatched it on its killing errands but maintained no active contact until it returned to him and he returned it to the Other Side."

"You mean he puts it back to sleep? Something like that?"

"Except tonight," Hania said.

"You want to fill me in on that?" the marshal asked.

"Tonight he has experienced some difficulty in restraining it. In fact..."

"What?" Thorn chipped in.

"I think he may have lost control. In which case we must hurry."

"Hurry where, exactly?" Ruggles asked.

"This way," Hania answered, pointing, and then nudged his Appaloosa pony to an all-out gallop.

"Terrific," Ruggles said, spurring his bay mare into hot pursuit. "We're rushing off to somewhere that we've never been, to kill some Yaqui that we've never seen before, and there may be a giant demon waiting for us."

"That's about the size of it," Thorn granted.

"Do you have a lot of nights like this?" the lawman asked.

"More than I care to think about," Gideon answered.

"And you've managed to survive them all?"

"So far," Thorn said. And then again as if for emphasis. "At least, so far."

Gideon was just about to ask Hania how much farther they would have to ride when the old Yaqui spoke up on his own to say, "We're nearly there."

"I don't see anything," Brett Ruggles said. "No giants, anyway."

"It has already gone," Hania answered back.

"You feel that do you?"

"If it still remained," the Yaqui said, "it would be coming for us now."

"Okay," the lawman said. "I guess that's comforting but still—"

"I smell woodsmoke," said Gideon. "Another thirty, forty yards at most."

They rode on silently from there, the white men with their hands on guns until Ruggles told his companions, "Over there." He pointed. "Something on the ground but I can't make it out."

They trailed the thin smoke from a dead or dying campfire to a patch of ground that had been cleared for camping. Reaching it, the three reined in, surveying clumps of something scattered out before them over eight or ten square yards.

"Looks like we came too late," Thorn said.

The objects strewn before them, seen up close by wan moonlight, were bloody fragments of at least two human bodies. They'd been clad in buckskin at some point but most of it was stripped away now. Thorn counted two sets of arms, the same of legs. Aside from the dismemberment, two torsos had been torn and trampled, one of them without a head attached or anywhere in sight. The second's head was twisted half a turn from normal, face down in the sand, which spared them having to examine ravaged features.

"Are you gonna say the *diablero* did this?" Ruggles asked Hania, nearly choking on the question.

"Yes," the shaman answered. "It has broken free of man's control."

"Which one of these was Cha-time?" Gideon asked.

Dismounting, Hania moved closer to examine the remains. After a moment, he pointed at the headless trunk. Said, "This one."

Off beyond the sundered bodies, Thorn had seen two twisted heaps of buckskin, *tipis* that were beaten down, most likely after Cha-time and Chu'a met their grisly ends. That came as no surprise but one of them was *moving* now, as if some animal was trapped inside when it collapsed.

"Heads up!" he warned the others. "Something's still alive here."

Hania moved forward, almost sprightly now, hands empty as he told his two companions, "There is no more danger. Do not fire."

Still, Thorn and Ruggles each had guns in hand as Hania drew back the rumpled buckskin to reveal a woman cringing on all fours, choking on silent tears.

"Come out, child," Hania advised her. "You have nothing more to fear."

He helped the woman to her feet and led her back to where Ruggles and Gideon were just dismounting from their steeds, uncocking pistols, and returning them to holsters.

"So, who's this?" the marshal asked.

"Your name, child?" Hania inquired.

Thorn could plainly see that she was not a child; in fact, her buckskin outfit snug enough to show ripe curves beneath it.

"Ahote," the woman said.

"You were Cha-time's woman," Hania observed, a statement rather than a question, answered with a jerky nod.

"Where has the *diablero* gone?" Hania asked.

Instead of answering, Ahote pointed back the way they'd come, southwestward. Ruggles cursed and scrambled back into his saddle.

"Come on then," he told the other two. "We must have missed it somehow riding out."

"It travels on the wind," Hania said. "But wait. Before we go, I must locate the tools Cha-time used for conjuring."

"Well make it snappy," Ruggles said. "We're already behind the game."

And Gideon, in fact, was moved to wonder if they were too late.

Riding back to Hades, Thorn was driven by a brooding fear that he and his companions would arrive too late. His knowledge of the *diablero* was distinctly limited but logic and his years of personal experience suggested that no mortal horse—even a stallion with the strength and speed of Shadow—could compete with any spirit of the supernatural.

If it was bound for Hades on a mission of destruction, they were far behind.

And what could any of them do to stop it if and when they finally arrive?

Gideon's mind was racing faster than his stallion's hooves across the open desert, back toward Hades, which would still be reeling from the loss of merchants, husbands, and assorted other townsmen. That left women and children on their own, in some households, unless they'd been invited in by friends and neighbors while their lives were in turmoil.

And now, if Hania was right in his surmise, danger was rapidly descending on them, bent on finishing the mission of annihilation.

Could the old shaman stop the *diablero* before that occurred? Gideon didn't know, but he had seen firsthand that ordinary bullets, even in profusion, had no impact on the demon. And if it were truly raised from fire, as Hania maintained, there was no reason to believe that flames would be effective in deterring it. The town lay open, at its mercy—if, that is, Ahote's guess about the monster's destination was correct.

If not, they could be chasing it till doomsday and that moment might not be far off.

As if reading his thoughts, Brett Ruggles raised his voice to ask, "What do we do when we get back to town?"

"Depends on if the *diablero*'s there or not," Thorn answered.

"If it is?"

"Find some way to buy time and let Hania work his medicine," Gideon said.

"And how might we do that, pray tell?"

"Beats me," Thorn said and let it go at that.

When they were still two miles from Hades, Thorn made out a glow on the horizon up ahead and recognized it as the light of leaping flames. One building in particular was burning brightly, Mercy Baptist's modest spire raised like a torch above the arid plain and beckoning them on toward destiny.

FOURTEEN

HADES

The *diablero* raged in silent exultation as it swept across the desert waste toward distant lights from town. There was a heady sense of liberation from its contest with the Yaqui shaman who had raised it and directed its attacks at scattered farms but now the hell-spawn drew strength from its independence, casting off the shackles that had held it back.

It was prepared to be about its true work now, ridding the land of interlopers on its own behalf and never mind the petty animus of one man who sought glory for himself by wielding a demonic puppet he was fool enough to think he could control.

The *diablero* had enjoyed destroying his controller and the shaman's friend as much as it had relished killing any of the white men slaughtered previously. More, in fact, because the shaman's blood had power of its own, absorbed upon consumption to enhance the demon's potency upon this earthly plain. The Yaqui's zeal would travel with the *diablero,* in a way, but not as its original possessor had surmised. His strength and vitriol remained but only as a kind of fuel, minus the ability to order any actions on the demon's part.

With half a mile to go before he reached the town of Hades, squatting in the night as if awaiting sacrifice, the *diablero* could already scent its various inhabitants—some watchful, others cowering.

No matter.

Nothing that they planned or hoped to do could save them from the fate ordained and rapidly approaching through the night.

Still, when the *diablero* reached the posted outskirts of the town, it paused sniffing the night once more, then stepped across the impotent imaginary line that residents of Hades once imagined kept them safe from harm. It knew the man who had attempted to attack the Yaqui reservation —not by name but by his self-important status as a holy man among the whites who normally offered suggestions in exchange for cash until the threat to his community became too obvious for him to shelter in his church. Anger and fear had merged to call him out, demanding that he join the dirty work himself, and he had paid for it, his sundered corpse discarded on the battleground.

And yet the house he'd built for a supposed divinity who challenged older, wiser gods for ultimate supremacy remained a monument the *diablero* could not tolerate. It would be first to fall before the demon worked its way through town eliminating any other signs of life.

A solitary guard was posted on the city limits facing to the northwest. Whether word had reached him of the raiding party's massacre, the *diablero* could not say and did not care. Moving like early morning mist, it closed upon the rifleman, only becoming visible to him when it was close enough to reach out and enfold his head in fingers tipped with claws. One savage twist prevented the watchman from crying out, much less using the weapon in his hands. He dropped between the *diablero's* feet like laundry slipping from a clothesline and sprawled lifeless on the ground.

The way lay open now. The demon did not hesitate.

It could not read the lettering painted across the church façade but had no need of English training to pick out its target by the spire on top, the simple wooden cross mounted above its double doors facing the street.

The *diablero* did not breathe per se, though it could smell and utter sounds akin to snarling. On occasion, it could even shriek like what some white men called a banshee. As it rushed the church and climbed its steps, one of those battle cries escaped its throat and echoed down the central street of Hades.

Surging up the wooden risers sagging under its weight, the *diablero* smashed those doors apart and stooped to clear the lintel as it surged into the narthex, then moved on into the chapel proper. Someone had left candles burning near the altar and the demon sent their candelabra hurtling toward the curtains hung on each side of a stained glass window looking down upon the apse beyond.

In nothing flat, the curtains were on fire, flames leaping up the wall and lapping at the ceiling overhead. The *diablero* watched until they caught hold of the wood, blistered its fading paint, and started gnawing at the boards beneath. When the whole wall was blazing, with the stained glass portrait of a pallid Jesus praying in the garden of Gethsemane entirely wreathed by hungry light, the *diablero* turned and moved back down the central aisle between two rows of pews, out through the broken double doors and back into the night.

Once clear, it raised a bellow to the night and moved off down the length of Easy Street, seeking its prey.

Thorn reined in a hundred yards from the official borderline for Hades and dismounted, willing Shadow to remain in place as long as possible or run to save himself if Gideon had not returned within a reasonable time.

Brett Ruggles missed him, wheeled around, and asked Thorn, "What's this, now?"

"I'm going in on foot," Gideon said, "and fetch my mule out of the livery before the whole town burns."

"Thanks for the confidence," Ruggles muttered.

"It's no reflection on yourself," Thorn said, "but neither one of us can stop this thing ourselves, as far as I can see."

"So what am I supposed to do?"

"Just what we talked about. Take Hania, set up in town, and don't let anybody shoot him while he's working."

"Are you coming back?" the marshal asked him, sounding worried now.

"As soon as I get Belle clear if the *diablero* doesn't stop me first," Thorn said.

"All right. I hope to see you soon."

"Just do your best," Gideon said. "And if it spins out of control know when to run."

He watched the marshal and Hania gallop off toward town, then followed in their wake on foot. A few more buildings were in flames by then but there was no smoke coming from the livery as Thorn sprinted to reach it in the darkness streaked by firelight.

Monte Rifkin was on duty, watching Easy Street and trying without much success to calm the animals in residence as Gideon arrived. He raised a double-barreled shotgun, was about to use it when he recognized his latest customer and said, "I wasn't sure if I'd be seeing you again."

"It's touch and go," Thorn said. "I'm here for Belle right now, then coming back to help the marshal if I can. He's brought some somebody with him that might be of help."

"The Indian? I saw 'em riding past just now," said Rifkin.

"That's Hania. If you spot him later, doing something you don't understand, he's on your side," Thorn said.

"Okay if you say so. Need help packing your mule?" asked Rifkin.

"No, thanks. I can handle it," said Gideon.

He felt Belle beaming anxious thoughts at him as he approached her stall, disturbed by crackling flames and drifting smoke nearby, and the commotion farther down on Easy Street, where random gunfire popped and crackled in the night. Some bestial roaring sound nearly eclipsed the rest of it, while men were cursing, shouting, and a woman screamed.

Thorn didn't take long packing Belle and they were out of there, retreating toward the spot where he'd left Shadow waiting for them. On arrival, Gideon gave a simplistic explanation to the animals that were his longtime friends and traveling companions, taking precious moments to unburden Belle, and set the packs beside her on the ground, to leave her unencumbered if she had to flee without him.

If he didn't make it back to join them later, they would have to get by on their own but Thorn kept that bit to himself.

That done, Winchester in his hand, Gideon started back into the hellscape Hades had become.

Arnold Primm had listened while his helper, Todd Mulaney, laid out what he'd seen outside of town, the posse led by Pastor Blake demolished and annihilated by some kind of giant that was visible and yet unclear, whatever that meant. They'd been starting on a batch of rough pine caskets when the marshal and his new friend all in black rode out again, this time with what appeared to be an aged Native tribesman mounted on an Appaloosa pony, riding hell for leather back the way they'd come, headed northwest of town.

By then, Hades was in an uproar, women and their children wailing over husbands, fathers, who had ridden off with Blake and were not coming back in any form their loved ones recognized. Primm had agreed with Marshal Ruggles that collection of the dead could wait for morning since coyotes and the like shied from remains at other murder sites and it would be a shame to miss someone—or part of someone—while they labored in the dark.

Mulaney wasn't keen on going back, of course, after the nightmare he had witnessed, but another twenty-five cents for each body got him back on board. As far as how Primm would collect his own fee from a flock of widows or from angry townsmen was a riddle he would still have to resolve.

The marshal and his two companions had been gone a while when Arnold heard a shout of "Fire!" outside, immediately echoed by a chorus of the same, somebody calling for responders to the Mercy Baptist Church. Stepping outside, Primm saw men rushing off in that direction, firelight glinting from the chapel's windows, then a massive figure started down the street in his direction, turning all the would-be firefighters around.

Behind Primm, Todd Mulaney shouted, "It's that thing again! You need to clear out, Mr. Primm, while there's still time!"

That said, Todd bolted back inside the shop, returning seconds later with the rifle that he'd carried while accompanying Marshal Ruggles and Gideon Thorn to watch the massacre of Pastor Blake's abortive raid against the Yaqui reservation.

His attention torn between his young assistant and the creature striding down the length of Easy Street, Primm asked Mulaney, "Todd, what are you doing?"

"This is my town, too, sir," Mulaney answered back. "I may not be worth much but I can fight!"

"And how did that work out for all those we've been building caskets for?" Primm asked.

"Don't matter," Todd replied. "I let it scare me off the first time and I figure once is plenty."

Seeing the determination on Mulaney's face, Primm did not bother arguing against his ill-considered plan. "Just keep your head down if you can," he said, then doubled back inside his shop.

Primm kept a gun there, like most other residents of Hades had at home, inside their shops, or both. He cherished no illusions that the Colt would stop whatever was proceeding down the street in his direction, putting other townsfolk on the run, nor did he plan to try.

The undertaker had not lived this long by courting trouble, much less of the killing kind. He counted on accommodation to get by in business and in life or lying low when there was no accommodation to be had. Right now, he figured, was a time to run and hide himself away, praying the grim invader would pass by, ignoring him, and move along.

If that made Arnold Primm a coward, he could live with it.

His main challenge tonight would be survival and, if Hades fell or burned to ash around him, he would make himself as small as possible to hostile eyes, praying he could become invisible. That was the way a sane man stayed alive when faced with insane circumstances he could not control.

If he could only hang on, somehow, until sunrise, things might be all right.

Brett Ruggles rode directly to his office and dismounted, did not tie his bay mare to the hitching rail out front as usual but left it free to run away if it felt so inclined. An impulse had come over him as he arrived outside the jail—an image of himself riding on through the heart of Hades, out the other side, and off into the night—but stubborn duty stopped him short of turning tail.

Goddamn responsibility! he thought and nearly laughed aloud as he pushed through the office door, crossed to the gun rack on the wall behind his desk, and started loading up his pockets with spare ammunition for his Winchester.

Not that the piece would do him any earthly good.

The *diablero* had already proved that as it ravaged Pastor Blake's sad troop of vigilantes but the marshal knew he had to try something while Hania was fooling with his medicine and Thorn was watching over him.

He chose the highest ground remaining in Hades after

the church caught fire and started to implode. Shoving into the Continental Hotel's lobby, Ruggles found no clerk on duty, calculating he had either run away by now—or worse, maybe had ridden out with Blake's late raiders, lying dead outside of town, and waiting for a pickup by the undertaker that might never come. The marshal clomped upstairs, his breathing labored, shouting on each floor along the way for any tenants still inside to hit the street and find a better hiding place but nobody responded to his calls.

The hotel's roof was flat and accessed by a ladder on the top floor, with a service hatch that folded back onto tarred shingles. Moving in a crouch to the roof's northwest corner, overlooking Easy Street, he knelt and watched the *diablero* or whatever tromping down the middle of the thoroughfare, a few shopkeepers firing at it from their stores or from apartment windows overhead.

For all their impact on the striding thing, those bullets might as well have been stray grains of sand blown on the restless desert wind. The *diablero* didn't even seem to notice them, its red eyes sweeping left to right and back again, grumbling louder than any sounds of gunfire, while it watched and waited for a foolish shooter to reveal himself outside.

The first to do so—obviously more courageous than he was intelligent, or maybe drunk by now—was Dave Kilgallen, owner of The Prairie Dog saloon. He burst onto the sidewalk through his barroom's swinging doors, holding a sawed-off Greener coach gun that he used to maim unruly pistol-packing customers from time to time, and leaned against one of the upright beams supporting his joint's wooden awning, lining up his shot from there.

Dave took his time, firing one barrel first, then weighing

its impact—nothing—before he let the other charge of buckshot fly. That would have killed a normal man and must have hit the *diablero,* although Ruggles could not swear to it from his high vantage point. Without a break in stride, the creature veered off to its right, reaching a long arm out to grab Kilgallen as he struggled to reload his scattergun.

It was too late for Dave to change his mind about being a hero, then, as massive fingers closed around his head and lifted him, the *diablero* hanging on as it performed a kind of whip-crack motion and Kilgallen's body flopped into the middle of the street, minus its skull.

That part, the creature shoved into its gaping maw as if it were devouring popcorn by the handful, crunching bones and all between its ragged teeth, blood streaming down its chin.

Brett Ruggles felt his sparse lunch, long forgotten, trying to escape his stomach but he kept it down by force of will alone. The nauseating moment passed and then he raised his Winchester and sighted down its barrel, triggering a shot into one of the *diablero*'s eyes.

The thing looked up at him, blinked once, then almost seemed to smile as it crossed Easy Street, marching toward the hotel.

Ellis Flynn observed the carnage through the office window of the *Hades Flame,* watching the biggest story of his journalistic life unfold. He scribbled notes in shorthand on a notepad, knowing that he was not likely to forget a single second of the nightmare being played out along Easy Street.

But would he live to print it? And if so, would anyone

outside of Hades take a single word of what he wrote as being true?

Unlike the town's marshal, Flynn could not manage to contain his supper as he witnessed Dave Kilgallen's death. No, it was worse than that. The Prairie Dog's proprietor had been decapitated, with his head consumed, mere yards from where Flynn stood in darkness, watching, pencil scratching over foolscap paper to record the ghastly scene.

A rifle shot rang out from somewhere to the newsman's right, across the street and elevated from it. Swiveling in that direction, Flynn saw someone—was it Marshal Ruggles—aiming from the Continental's rooftop for another try. Like other bullets fired against the giant creature since it ransacked Mercy Baptist and left the church in flames, those bullets seemed to have no impact on the towering invader, either passing through it somehow, or perhaps just wasted by a hasty trigger-pull.

Not Dave Kilgallen's shotgun, though.

Flynn had observed the aftermath of shootings at The Prairie Dog and knew Kilgallen never missed his mark with that Greener, its barrels cut down to the minimum a shooter could endure without the muzzle flashes scorching his forehand. If two full buckshot charges could not stop the thing, or even slow it down, Flynn had to wonder if his town had any hope at all.

Just stay alive and get the facts all written down, Flynn thought. If there was nothing left of Hades come first light tomorrow, he could find another printing press somewhere or even make the ride to Tucson, try to sell his story to the *Citizen* for cash enough to come back and rebuild, or maybe start up on a small scale somewhere else.

That was, assuming that the *Tucson Citizen* would touch his story with a ten-foot pole, much less put any credence in the tale, rather than simply mocking him as a demented fool.

"Forget that," Ellis muttered to himself. "Just take it one step at a time."

And step one was surviving if he had a hope of doing so.

If forced to bet right then, Flynn would have said the odds were slim to none.

The *diablero* could not read the Continental Hotel's sign and did not care whatever message it conveyed. The latest enemy to challenge it was on the building's roof, which posed a problem of logistics even if the demon did not comprehend that human term.

It had the strength to crash in through the hotel's entryway but, once inside, constricted space would make its movements awkward, slowing progress to a crawl. It knew nothing of stairs per se but realized there must be narrow corridors inside, some means of climbing from the ground floor upward, and the damage it inflicted in the process might well bring the structure crashing down upon it.

Not that falling timber could destroy the *diablero*, much less injure it, but in the time it took to force its way through tumbling rubble, its intended target on the hotel's roof might either slip away or else be killed somehow by accident. Neither outcome was satisfactory tonight.

The *diablero* wanted to enjoy each kill it made with its own hands and fangs.

It paused to glance back along Easy Street, beheld the Mercy Baptist church in flames, and realized there was another way to force its adversary down from his high perch. At least two lamps were burning in the hotel lobby, either one of them sufficient to ignite the building, send fire racing upward toward the desert sky.

In that case, the offending rifleman would have a choice of coming down somehow to face his enemy or staying on the roof to be incinerated on a funeral pyre. In either case, his death would be the *diablero*'s doing, not some random stroke of chance.

And that would be enough to satisfy it while it hunted other humans in their shops and homes.

Snarling, it smashed in through the Continental's tall front door and reached the nearest lamp, hurling it twenty feet to strike an oak wall. Flames instantly exploded from it, spreading to the carpet, racing up the stairs, and crackling toward the floors above.

The *diablero* backed out of that conflagration, raised its glowing eyes, and settled in to wait.

Hania needed fire to work his medicine and Hades had no shortage of potential sources now. For safety's sake, he chose a heap of burning rubble that had once been someone's hardware store, dragged burning boards into the thoroughfare, and knelt before them, opening the buckskin pouch of powders he had gathered from the shambles of Cha-time's campsite earlier.

In all his years, Hania had not summoned any life form from the Other Side but he knew all the rituals his ancestors had handed down by word of mouth. Granted, undoing someone else's magic spell would be more difficult, made doubly so after the *diablero* had dispatched its earthly master but Hania knew he was the last, best hope for what remained of Hades and the white domain beyond.

A world he hated which had never given any Yaqui tribesman anything but pain.

Why should he struggle to preserve it, when by simply doing nothing he might help to bring it crashing down for good?

Because, in that case, Hania knew he would be complicit and would place his soul at mortal risk.

Crouching before the fire he'd gathered on the edge of Easy Street, Hania loosed the buckskin pouch from his belt, spilling its colored granules into the palm of one hand. With a sweeping motion, chanting softly to the background noise of crackling flames, he dumped the powder on the burning pile of lumber and began to sway, the volume of his voice increasing, eyes glazed by the bright rainbow of fire rising before him.

How long would it take to draw the *diablero* back to him and to its own demise, assuming that Hania had the power to achieve his goal?

The old Yaqui had no idea, except to realize that these might be the final moments of his life.

Thorn knew the Continental was a lost cause from the moment that the *diablero* crashed into its lobby and the hotel started burning from the ground up. There was time, just barely, for him to retreat downstairs, enter his room, and exit with his Sharps rifle and satchel filled with clothes before retreating to the roof once more.

From there, he'd seen a ladder down the back wall of the Continental, doubling as a fire escape and service access to the roof. No other tenants were evacuating as Thorn started down toward ground level, presumably because they'd vacated before the *diablero* turned up in their midst and started wreaking havoc through the heart of town.

He reached the desert flats behind the Continental, smoke roiling from windows on the first and second floors now, doubling back in the direction that the *diablero* had advanced from. Thorn had no firm plan in mind beyond protecting Hania while the shaman did everything within his power to eradicate the demon or at least divert it from continuing the destruction of Hades.

And if Hania could not stop the demon cold, what then?

Thorn did not have a clue.

In Southern California, soon after he met Dinah Pilcher, a Native collaborator's spell had managed to prevent the second coming of a savage deity from long ago. That didn't mean the same procedure would accomplish anything tonight, in Arizona Territory, but Thorn knew that bullets, flame, and other earthly weapons would not do the trick.

If Hania fell short, Gideon didn't want to think about what that might mean for any victims in the future. He assumed that Christian prayers were out since Pastor Blake had met disaster on his raid against the Yaquis reservation after promising his comrades God was on their side.

Jogging back toward the last point where he had glimpsed Hania at the northern end of Easy Street, Thorn hoped *something* would work to halt the *diablero's* rampage or at least postpone it until some other solution could be found.

And failing that, he knew the town named after Hell itself would be eradicated from the map.

Brett Ruggles knew it was a waste of time to shoot the *diablero* with his Winchester but took the chance regardless. Wasted time and ammunition it turned out, his bullet striking near the center of the creature's back and having no impact at all as far as he could tell.

Mere seconds earlier Ruggles had watched the Continental Hotel caving in upon itself, its floors pancaking as they fell, sparks flying on a cloud of smoke, some settling on nearby shops that started smoldering on their slow way to immolation.

No one made it out of the hotel's front door while Ruggles watched, although the backdoor offered an alternative escape path. Focusing as best he could, the marshal saw no trace of Thorn up on the roof before it started tumbling down into the pyre. He hoped the man in black had managed to descend using the Continental's fire escape but there was no time to cross over Easy Street and find out for himself.

The town was dying right in front of him and Ruggles could do nothing now but stand and watch—or maybe sacrifice himself, a hopeless suicide, charging the creature from behind with no hope he could bring it down alone.

To Hell with that, he thought and almost laughed aloud.

If Hades had not been transformed into a kind of Hell on Earth, it was the closest Ruggles ever hoped to come.

Advancing toward Hania and his crude campfire, bright-colored flames leaping from splintered planks of wood, Ruggles spotted Gideon Thorn emerging from an alley to his right, crossing Easy Street in the same direction the marshal was headed. Thorn carried two rifles, and while logic told Ruggles those weapons would do no more good against the *diablero* than his own Winchester, he still felt better knowing that the man in black would stand beside him to the bitter end.

Whatever that end proved to be, Ruggles was braced to play his part in it and go down fighting with no realistic hope that he would come out on the other side of it alive.

Hania saw the two white men converging on him, motioning impatiently for them to get behind him and avoid obstructing contact with the *diablero*. There was no time left to answer any of their questions, the old shaman was busy chanting in his tribal tongue and making mystic gestures with his hands above the colored flames he'd kindled with Cha-time's magic powders.

For long moments, he was worried that the *diablero* would not hear his call or answer to it since Cha-time's would have been the only human voice it recognized. Already more than halfway down the length of Easy Street, it seemed to be ignoring him, intent on wreaking havoc upon Hades and its residents, veering off-course to hound and trample those who crossed its path.

But then, when the old Yaqui shaman had begun to doubt himself, the *diablero* paused, perked up its pointed ears, and slowly turned to face where Hania crouched behind the fire, flanked by two riflemen clutching their useless guns. It snarled—a visceral, unnerving sound—and slowly started back along the thoroughfare, advancing cautiously upon Hania as he warbled ancient chants and songs passed down through generations of his tribe.

Whether enraged or simply curious—Hania could not say—the demon rapidly increased its pace, ignoring stray townsmen who veered across its path. Hania realized he had the *diablero's* full attention now but drawing it toward him was one thing. Killing it, if that were even possible, was something vastly different.

In fact, the Yaqui shaman reckoned that the best he could achieve was sending it back from the earthly plane to wherever it brooded on the Other Side, waiting to once again be summoned forth. If he could manage *that,* at least, Hania might consider that his quest had been successful after all.

And if the effort cost his life...well, that meant one less shaman with the power to evoke the *diablero* and dispatch it on another killing spree.

"What's happening?" Brett Ruggles asked.

Hania hissed to silence him, uncertain how the white lawman would take it and no longer caring. He had eyes and ears only for the demonic entity before him, drawing ever closer, stride by loping stride.

Hania chanted louder, passed his hands directly through the colored flames without feeling their heat. His flesh and whatever became of it this night no longer mattered. Leaning forward, nearly shouting at the *diablero* now, he issued orders that Hania knew might fall upon deaf ears while he was trampled into pulp.

But if the demon heard him, if his incantations reached into its blighted soul, there still might be a chance.

Rising on shaky legs, Hania stood before the *diablero,* less than half its height but standing ramrod straight, his hands raised overhead and making passes through the smoky air. At the last moment, as the creature towered over him, bending to reach down for him with its massive hands, Hania kicked the campfire, putting all his strength behind it, spraying sparks and blackened shards of wood across the *diablero's* legs.

Gideon Thorn raised one arm up to shield his eyes from flying embers as Hania kicked the remnants of his fire a second time, extinguishing its flames while spewing ash and dirt across the *diablero*'s lower limbs. Instead of lunging at the shaman, ripping him apart, the specter froze in place, a look of consternation on its savage face, its snarling silenced as it started down at the Yaqui shaman from on high.

"What's going on?" Ruggles demanded, standing at his side.

Thorn, having no idea on the matter, offered no reply but waited to find out what happened next.

Before his startled eyes, the *diablero* took a halting backward step, then made as if to rush upon Hania and destroy the old man where he stood. Before it could complete that crushing move, however, Gideon beheld its image waver in reflected firelight from the Mercy Baptist Church and other buildings it had set ablaze along the length of Easy Street. It seemed to tremble, substance fading in and out like a desert mirage before it surged back to a semblance of solidity and took another long stride toward Hania on the far side of his scattered fire.

One stride—and then no more.

"My God!" Brett Ruggles blurted out and Thorn knew that the *diablero's* shimmering before his eyes was no mere trick of light and shadow. Ruggles saw it, too. As tall and powerful as it had been a moment earlier, the demon's form was wavering, became nearly transparent for a heartbeat, then solidified once more into a thing resembling flesh and blood, raising a howl that shook the windows in whatever buildings still remained standing in Hades.

Lurching forward in a clumsy rush, the *diablero* stopped short as if it had run into a stout brick wall. From there, it toppled slowly forward, Thorn and Ruggles edged backward to avoid it as the giant plunged face-foremost toward Hania and the ground on which he stood.

Gideon cried a warning to the shaman but Hania did not seem to hear him. Standing fast, arms raised and open as if to embrace his enemy, the Yaqui did not flinch or cringe before the *diablero* as it toppled onto him.

And that was not the strangest part of it. Instead of simply crushing its opponent like an insect, the demonic entity fell *through* Hania, through the unpaved surface of the thoroughfare, and vanished altogether in a roiling cloud of dust. Hania, for his part, remained upright for several seconds longer, then his legs gave out beneath him and he crumpled to the ground that had consumed his enemy.

Gideon was crouched beside him in another instant, lifting the old Yaqui to a limp sitting position, Brett Ruggles beside him, lending aid. The wide-eyed marshal peered around them as if fearing that the *diablero* might emerge once more and crush them all.

But there was nothing left of it except, perhaps, a lingering stench of corruption on the night air, vying with the smell of drifting woodsmoke from establishments the thing had set on fire before it fell.

Thorn held Hania, raised one hand to seek a pulse beneath the Yaqui's jaw but found none. The old man's skin felt clammy to his touch, already cooling in the night air as if Thorn had come upon him thirty minutes to an hour after death.

Hania's eyes were open, staring at the night sky, until Ruggles closed them with a gentle pressure from his hand.

Turning to Thorn, he asked, "You want to tell me what just happened here?"

"You saw the same as I did," Gideon replied. "Hania stopped it somehow and the *diablero* took him with it."

"Took him where?" the marshal pressed.

"Beats me," Thorn answered back. "For now, let's just be thankful that it's gone."

"And what if it comes back?"

"I wouldn't count on that," Thorn said. "But keep your fingers crossed."

EPILOGUE

HADES: SEPTEMBER 9, 1877

Thorn finished off the letter, read it through, and satisfied himself that it was adequate for posting home to Boston. He had written—

Dearest Dinah,

I hope this finds you well and that you will accept my most sincere apology for failing to answer your last letter in more timely fashion. Matters have been hectic here in Arizona Territory, with the town of Hades—yes, you read that rightly—verging on disaster until they were finally resolved last night.

Of course, you know from personal experience how that so often goes, and I cannot pretend the town or its small population managed to emerge unscathed from the experience. I shall impart full details if you wish, when next we correspond or speak in person, but for now I'll simply say that it was reminiscent of events from San Diego County when we met for the first time, some fourteen months ago.

How long it seems since then, the roads that we have

followed and the perils we have shared. In this case, I decided that your physical recovery would not be hastened by involvement in another struggle to survive forces beyond the scope of "normal" life. That was my unilateral decision, made with your best interest at heart, and if my choice offends you, I apologize once more.

Before this letter reaches you, you may have heard some intimations of what's happened here in Pima County, though as you might readily expect, the facts will certainly be filtered by the press to put the minds of common folk at ease. One newsman—Ellis Flynn, publisher of the Hades Flame*—observed some of the incidents first-hand but I suspect he will have difficulty publishing the story without meddling by the Powers That Be in Tucson and the capital at Phoenix.*

When we meet again, I will of course share all the details with you, holding nothing back, if that should be your wish. Conversely, if you should prefer to hear no more, I would find no fault with your choice. Until that day, I wish you all the best and send fondest regards to Obi, who I trust has made you feel at home on Beacon Hill.

Sincerely,
Gideon

There had been more to say, of course—much more—but Thorn had not committed it to paper, understanding that a letter sometimes went astray for weeks or months on end and might, in fact, never arrive at its intended destination.

If that happened, his next trip to Boston would be a surprise for Dinah Pilcher. As to what he might find when they met again at last...well, Gideon would simply have to wait and see.

He sealed the letter up inside an envelope, addressed it

to the Thorn mansion on Boston's stylish Beacon Hill, and looked around the spare bedroom he'd occupied in Marshal Ruggles's home, ensuring that he'd left nothing behind that might be needed on the trail. Ruggles was waiting for him in the parlor when Thorn finally emerged, wearing a rueful smile.

"You're certain I can't talk you into breakfast?" asked the lawman.

There'd been minor damage to O'Grady's in the chaos overnight but the establishment had come off better than Casa del Sol which wound up burning to the ground along with Thorn's hotel and both saloons. Gideon wondered what survivors of the fight would do for alcohol over the next few days but reckoned that the void would soon be filled by new proprietors, peddling new women and the same old booze.

In spite of monsters cropping up from time to time, he'd learned that life went on—at least for some.

"I'd best be on my way as planned," he told Ruggles. "Thanks for the bed last night."

"Hell, it's the least I could have done. I'd pay you something if I could but now the town's tapped out. No telling if I'll have a job tomorrow or the whole place will dry up and blow away."

"Don't count it out just yet," said Gideon. "From what I've seen, Hades endures."

The marshal laughed at that. "I guess that's right, although I'm not sure how to take it."

"Anyway you like," Gideon said.

"Where are you headed next?"

"My first stop is in Tucson," Thorn replied. "I've got a letter that needs posting and I'll likely take a couple days to sniff around, see what the aftermath of all this proves to be."

"And look for what comes next?"

Gideon thought of Dinah Pilcher and the endless road that stretched in front of him, wondering if it were time to travel east, or whether some new mystery would lead him off to yet another brush with sudden death.

"You never know," Thorn answered with a wistful smile. "I take things as they come."

A LOOK AT: WORMFOOD: A DARK COMEDY NOVEL (THE SUTTER FAMILY LEGACY OF EVIL BOOK 1)

Arch Cutter has a bad job—and it's about to get a hell of a lot worse. Sixteen, broke, and trapped in the rotting little town of Whitewood, California, Arch spends his days scraping grease off dishes at Fat Ernst's Bar & Grill, dreaming of escape. But when his corrupt boss forces him to do something truly filthy, Arch unwittingly unleashes an ancient horror buried deep beneath the valley.

Now the townsfolk of Whitewood are dying in unspeakable ways—devoured from the inside out by parasitic worms that turn human flesh into a buffet. As the infection spreads, old feuds ignite, blood flows freely, and the line between man and monster dissolves in a storm of shotgun blasts, bad decisions, and black magic.

If Arch doesn't find a way to stop the madness, the whole town will be crawling with death before sunrise.

Grindhouse gore meets small-town apocalypse in this darkly funny, stomach-churning horror that proves one thing for sure—everybody's dying to get out alive.

AVAILABLE NOW

THANK YOU

Thank you for taking the time to read *Warpath*. If you enjoyed it, please consider telling your friends or posting a short review. Word of mouth is an author's best friend and much appreciated.

Thank you.
Michael Newton

ABOUT THE AUTHOR

A California native, Michael Newton published over 215 books under his own name and various pseudonyms since 1977. He began writing professionally as a "ghost" for author Don Pendleton on the best-selling Executioner series. With 104 episodes published to date, Newton nearly tripled the number of Mack Bolan novels completed by creator Pendleton himself.

www.ingramcontent.com/pod-product-compliance
Lightning Source LLC
LaVergne TN
LVHW040218110826
845146LV00005B/1342

* 9 7 9 8 8 9 5 6 7 6 1 3 4 *